I0602905

YARA'S

A Novel

ANTHEM

Wagih Abu-Rish

RIVER GROVE
BOOKS

This book is a work of fiction. Names, characters, businesses, organizations, places, events, and incidents are either a product of the author's imagination or are used fictitiously. Any resemblance to actual persons, living or dead, events, or locales is entirely coincidental.

Published by River Grove Books
Austin, TX
www.rivergrovebooks.com

Copyright © 2024 Wagih Abu-Rish

All rights reserved.

Thank you for purchasing an authorized edition of this book and for complying with copyright law. No part of this book may be reproduced, stored in a retrieval system, or transmitted by any means, electronic, mechanical, photocopying, recording, or otherwise, without written permission from the copyright holder.

For permission to reproduce copyrighted material, grateful acknowledgment is made to the following:
A. Z. Foreman, Translator, Copyright Ó by A. Z. Foreman, from "The Lake" by Alphonse de Lamartine, from blog *Poems Found in Translation.* Used by permission.

Distributed by River Grove Books

Design and composition by Greenleaf Book Group
Cover design by Greenleaf Book Group and Riley Quinn

Publisher's Cataloging-in-Publication data is available.

Paperback ISBN: 978-1-63299-888-0

Hardcover ISBN: 978-1-63299-889-7

eBook ISBN: 978-1-63299-890-3

First Edition

*To all those who confess to being ethically
and socially subconsciously biased and proceed
to consciously correct such character flaws.*

Contents

*Human beings are subconsciously biased and only
their upbringing, education, and intellectual exercise
raise them to a level whereby they recognize their failing
and admit to it, in order to consciously correct it.*

Main Characters

YARA SHAHIN—Main character

AYMAN SHAHIN—Yara's father

NADER SHAHIN—Yara's brother

JEAN GARNIER—French cultural attaché in Jordan

ANNETTE ALLARD—French sponsor of Yara

ANTOINE ALLARD—Annette's husband

JEAN PIERRE ALLARD—Annette's son

MARCO—Honduran student at Berea College

MOENS—Yara's nemesis at Berea and Harvard

BERNARD—Yara's boyfriend while at Berea

RACHEL SHAHAK—Yara's friend at U. of Michigan and roommate at Harvard

JOSEPH SHAHAK—Rachel's father

JAMEELA—Yara's second roommate at Harvard

JAMAL—Jameela's brother

KHALIL—Yara's cousin

REVEREND PFEIFER—Methodist minister

AMANDA PFEIFER—Reverend Pfeifer's wife

PART I

Amman, 1963

Chapter 1

My name is Yara, a name chosen for me by my father. Shortly after he got engaged to my mother, Amina, he shared with her that he wanted to call his first baby girl Yara. He thought it was simple, yet flowing and expressive. It means "baby butterfly."

My father, Ayman Shaheen, had the greatest influence on me throughout my first fifteen years of life. Despite the fact that we lived in a Palestinian refugee camp near Amman, Jordan, I felt we were lucky and happy. By camp standards, we lived comfortably, in a two-bedroom, one-bathroom house. My mother told my father that she always liked the name Yara but did not know it meant "baby butterfly." He then asked her to choose a name for a boy. She thought for a while and told him that she could not make up her mind between Kareem or Nader. She told me that she later chose Nader.

I felt ours was a lovely home. There was a gallery in the middle, with the living room on one side and the two bedrooms on the other. Originally the bathroom had been at the end of the gallery, but my father decided to open up the space and moved the bathroom behind the bedroom I shared with Nader.

My father was a French language teacher who developed a love for the French language by sheer accident. It all came about unexpectedly. It happened many years ago, when I was fifteen. The French educational attaché in Amman visited the camp to talk to the Arabic language teachers. He did not invite any of the English language teachers. The French and the British had competed for centuries all throughout the Middle East, and everyone guessed that this was intentional, including my father.

After applying, around twenty were invited to the meeting. There, the attaché expressed his regrets that there was not a single French language teacher at the camp. He offered a full one-year scholarship to tutor one of the twenty to become a French language teacher. My father was the only volunteer. The other nineteen thought it was unrealistic to master the French language in one year. So did my father, yet he welcomed the challenge. He was chosen on the spot.

Little did the other nineteen know how lucrative the scholarship would end up being. It was way beyond my father's expectations. It entailed a trip to France to study in the city of Besançon for ten months. Father grew skeptical when he heard that the course was less than a year long. The attaché managed to partially soothe his concerns when he explained that once he returned from the course in Besançon, the embassy would provide him with a hands-on teacher for three months to walk him through how to teach French in the refugee camp.

My father told us he was expecting the French would pay him his $150 monthly, in lieu of his regular salary. To my father's surprise, the attaché informed him that instead he would be paid $400 a month, on top of free room and board. The attaché then said, "With this program, there can be two reasons behind any failure. The first would be your dislike of the French language and the second if you happen to be a lazy student. We wouldn't spend this kind of money without being sure that you have every opportunity to succeed. The camp director provided us with your background, and I am very confident you will perform exceedingly well."

My father said nothing; his face must have exhibited an expression of lingering doubt, since he didn't know anything about the program, nor had he ever heard of Besançon.

That evening, after he came back from grading some exams, he summoned the family. My brother, Nader, and I sat on either side of him, and my mother sat facing him. He told us then that he was going to be away for ten months learning French in France. It was a bit of a shock to all of us. My mother was worried about his monthly salary of $150. My father then explained about the $400 monthly stipend; with that, according to the French attaché, he could easily save $300 a month.

"I will send you $150 a month, and I will save another $150," he told my mother. He then explained that when he returned to teach French, he would get $100 monthly from the French embassy on top of his $150 salary.

I could see the expression on my mother's face changing. I thought that she would finally be able to buy missing utensils and a new dining table. She smiled, looked at my father, and then said, "May God keep you." My father took her hand and kissed it to show his appreciation for her understanding and support. Kissing a wife's hand is a most uncommon gesture for an Arab man. My father was not affluent, yet he was refined, articulate, and learned. Above all, he was socially liberated and sensitive, especially by Middle Eastern standards. Most of his informal education was through his extensive reading of Arabic books. Occasionally, he would read an English book, such as some of the Shakespearean plays.

He used to complain that it took four times as long to read the same works in English. He said it with a sense of satisfaction rather than that of complaint. He liked the English language but found it less versatile than Arabic. He used to describe Arabic as "a verb-based language with a plethora of rich derivatives."

His choice to go to France was met with his own skepticism. He convinced himself that the French were only interested in any kind of camp presence for a French language teacher, and that they felt the current lack of this was an insult that they needed to rectify any which way, as soon as possible. He never expected to become much more than a rudimentary French language teacher.

Within two months, he was off to France, after giving my mother $150 for the month. It was sixty dollars more than he usually gave her to manage the financial affairs of the household. The usual balance from the $150 was kept by my father to pay for our books and to buy health insurance coverage. We did not own a car. My father owned a bicycle, which required very little maintenance.

It felt strange not having my father at home. My mother was mostly resigned to his absence and was appreciative of the extra stipend. My brother didn't care. He was not as close to my father as I was. He wasn't like me—being nurtured socially and culturally, especially in the pleasures of reading Arabic literature.

Within a few days, my mother and I started talking about Father's expected first letter from France. It didn't reach us until four weeks after his departure, although he had written it one day after his arrival in Besançon. It was his first letter to us ever: Before then, he'd never been away alone for more than four days.

He started by writing "My love, you would not believe what has happened in one single day in Besançon. A guide ushered me to the office of the principal. The guide either did not speak English or pretended not to speak English. He signaled that I needed to knock on the door. When the principal opened the door, he must have recognized me from my picture on my application. He shook my hand and said in English, 'From this moment on, you have only one choice: You must communicate by speaking French, as much as you can, for no one will answer you if you use any other language.' It has been less than twenty-four hours, and I have managed to survive. I have already picked up four sentences and around two dozen words. For me, now, the most important word is *toilette*."

My father's letters kept coming at the rate of one a week. Within one month, we felt that his mood was starting to get more optimistic. By the end of the second month, he was very hopeful that he could learn French within the prescribed ten months. The biggest surprise came after the third month. He said in his letter "Believe it or not, I can now not only speak French but speak it reasonably well. I don't know how it happened. Somehow, things have come together, and sentences started to be formed in my head without much effort. I really can speak French now. Unbelievable!"

I looked at my mother, and she looked at me. Was this really true? Or had what the attaché told him about succeeding been right on the money? My beautiful and earthy mother said, "They say the French are very romantic since their language is very romantic," and stopped without saying anything else. I could tell she was wondering if my father would behave more romantically after learning French.

I said nothing. Being fifteen at the time, I didn't want to reveal what I was secretly reading about love and sex. I never brought such books and articles home. They were not mine in the first place. They belonged to Mira, my best friend. Her father worked in Saudi Arabia and could afford many things we could not. She was always considerate, and she shared most everything with me. Coincidently, my favorite romance reading was an Arabic book about a French author, *The Life and Loves of Alexandre Dumas*. In it, Dumas was described as a leading novelist and playwright who had more than forty romantic liaisons. I couldn't believe what I had read, especially the passion and sex entailed in these gorgeous relationships. There was one book I kept to myself and guarded with my life for one week, until I returned it to Mira: *The Return to Adolescence*. It was all about Indian sex acts and positions.

Four months after my father left, we got used to his absence. In the evening, instead of my father sharing his literary likes with me, I tried to share my knowledge with my mother. She was only an elementary school graduate. She quit school after Israel chose her village as a dump site and her family was forced to move to Amman to live with relatives. Yet, she managed to reconcile with her new, less fortunate setup. I wanted her to know more and enjoy more, although she seemed to be happy with what she had, especially after she married my father.

Every time I brought up a new intellectual subject to discuss with my mother, she resorted to the same refrain: "You are becoming a beautiful woman. It's true you are still young, but in two years you won't be. The young men will be eyeing you, and then soon one of them will summon the courage to tell his parents. They'll contact your father and ask to visit us. Hopefully, it will be a family we know and respect. Nowadays, it's difficult to know the real quality of people you don't know from before."

That theme was so much removed from any consideration of mine. I wanted to study and, hopefully, manage to go to university. I knew that my family couldn't afford to send me, yet I was still hopeful something could change.

Ten months and four days later, my father was back home, accompanied by none other than the French attaché. I was walking with Mira when I unexpectedly saw the two talking to each other. I wanted to run toward my father but paused to hear him speaking to the attaché in what sounded like flowing and possibly fluent French. I then ran toward him, and he kissed me four times, twice on each cheek. He introduced me to the attaché with those same French speech intonations. To my ears, it sounded perfect.

My father asked me to hurry up and tell my mother that the attaché was accompanying him home. I ran ahead of them. My mother didn't know how to react to the news. She was elated that my father was back but disturbed that our humble house was not up to par, despite having a new dining table. When the two of them entered the house, my father was off-balance. He didn't seem to know whether to hug Mother or what to do. The attaché nudged my father toward my mother, and he hugged her warmly.

We'd never experienced someone this important visiting us. It was awkward. The attaché looked around our living room and must have found it to be spartan. His quick glance at each piece of furniture revealed their age and worn condition. Before he left, he told my father that he was going to give him another thousand dollars to jazz things up, because he intended to bring other Frenchmen interested in the Palestinian cause to visit him. Notwithstanding our surprised looks and confusion, I couldn't believe my ears. Despite the situation, my father continued to speak French with the attaché with ease.

In the evening, my father explained things. He said that he started to speak French at first most grudgingly, and later with gusto, eighteen hours a day. "In the end, I forgot about Arabic all together," he said. "It was an amazing experience, and now I love the French language, much more than English."

After my mother and brother went to bed, my father insisted on reading me his favorite French poem, "The Lake," by Alphonse de Lamartine. He went through it slowly but repeated one stanza twice:

> *Recall the evening we sailed out in silence?*
> *On waves beneath the skies, afar and wide,*
> *Naught but the rowers' rhythmic oars we heard,*
> *Stroking your tuneful tide.*

Chapter 2

After my father returned from France, my mother developed a distinct radiant look. I was doubtful it had anything to do with any sexual transformation on the part of my father, but who knows. I knew that she stopped feeling the stress of running out of funds five days before the end of each month. Not only did she have enough, but she was saving between ten and eighteen dollars each month. After a year she had accumulated $183 dollars in savings. By then our house looked much nicer, after using nine hundred of the thousand given to us by the attaché.

One early morning, one of the camp policemen knocked at our door. He said that his captain in Amman had called to let us know that the French attaché was bringing two French tourists to visit my father. It so happened that my father was in bed that day, not feeling well. When my father heard about the visit, he had no intention of disappointing the attaché. He told the policeman that he was available to receive the attaché and his guests. My mother tried to convince my father to decline gracefully but to no avail. She and I both thought he didn't look good and needed to rest.

When the attaché arrived with his two guests, Mr. and Mrs. Allard, the three could tell that my father was not in good health.

They tried to leave, but my father insisted that they stay. I couldn't take it, looking at my father's pale face and listening to his labored breathing. I excused myself to go out. Within two minutes, my father and the attaché went out too and seemed to engage in a serious conversation, all in French. My father then took a piece of paper out of the inside pocket of his coat and showed it to the attaché. All I could hear and understand was "Oh, la, la," from the attaché. I knew it was an expression of surprise, sometimes pleasant and sometimes not so pleasant.

I could tell that the attaché was disturbed at what he heard. I was curious to know why the attaché was so surprised and why he and his guests left very shortly after such conversation. I was hoping that my father would share something with us, as I was especially concerned, but he did not. For the first time in my life, I waited for everyone to go to bed and then looked into the inside pocket of his jacket to find the report. It said that my father needed a heart operation as soon as possible. Despite the alarming news, I was at a loss as to whether or not to tell my mother. I decided not to until I could find a way to cover up how I'd found out.

To our surprise, the attaché and his guests were back two days later. They met in our living room and spoke in French. That evening, my father summoned the three of us and told us that he had to go into the hospital for a heart operation. My mother went berserk. She was instantly convinced that a heart operation meant a death sentence. My father had to calm her down and asked her to give him a chance to finish what he needed to say.

He said that he felt lucky that the French embassy volunteered to pay for most of the costs—80 percent—since they did not have a French hospital in Jordan. It was as far as they could go. My father continued explaining: "This attaché, Jean Garnier, is an angel, and he wants to help in coming up with the rest of the money. Mr. and Mrs. Allard have volunteered to pay the balance and offered to have Yara work at one of their two hotels in Paris, for our family to use the money to pay for the expenditures of this house while I am off work."

My mother jumped up from the chair and said, "Yara is a teenager. You don't mean she will be working in France!" When my father explained that he had only four hundred dollars left in savings, and that what the Allards were offering was generous, my mother simmered down and, without saying anything, seemed to accept my working in France during the three summer months. I didn't know how I felt. It was exciting but challenging, especially because I didn't speak any French.

I was confused and didn't know what to say or do. I decided to talk to Mira. This meant being willing to listen to her mostly off-balance advice, but I was craving any comforting company. When I told Mira about the offer to work in Paris, the first thing she asked was whether I could buy her a couple of dresses she had in mind. Her father couldn't find what she wanted in Saudi Arabia. By the time I finished talking to her, I couldn't tell if our conversation had been more soothing or irritating.

It took my mother and I a week to accept that the plan, as described by my father, was the only choice. For the next two months, I was apprehensive about what I would be doing in a place where I couldn't speak the language. In the end I told myself, *It can't be that bad.* Since the Allards knew everything about my father and me and were smart people, they wouldn't expect more than I could manage. My father had the procedure and came out of it a revived man.

When the time came for me to leave, I was heartened by the fact that Jean Garnier accompanied me to the airport. There, he gave me an envelope and gave a similar envelope to the head Air France flight attendant. He also gave me five hundred French francs. He told me that Mr. and Mrs. Allard were scheduled to meet me at the airport and that the five hundred francs were for taking a taxi to their main hotel, in case we somehow missed each other at the airport. It was more than enough.

Based on his written instructions, he assured me that Air France would facilitate things for me and wouldn't leave me stranded. When I got on the plane, the head flight attendant eased my worries by telling me that she would personally hand me over to the Allards and would help in case they didn't show up.

PART II
Paris and Kentucky, 1963–1968

Chapter 3

I was completely relieved to find that the Allards were waiting for me, with their seventeen-year-old son, Jean Pierre. Absorbed by our own challenges, my father had never asked the Allards about the makeup of their family. Annette Allard, the mother, was very welcoming. She kissed me on both cheeks, and after I shook hands with Antoine, the father, and Jean Pierre, Annette put her arms around me and walked me to their car.

She zigzagged me around the anxious passengers and airport employees all the way to the terminal door. She was the first person to open any door for me. Their large Citroen was waiting at the curb. Jean Pierre gave the luggage to the driver, and he opened the car door for me while Antoine opened the car door for Annette.

I was barely observing what was going on as my mind concentrated on Jean Pierre. It wasn't that I was attracted to him, although he was very handsome; it was mainly because he was my age and new to me. Annette noticed me looking at him. In response, she volunteered that they had only one son. I felt I needed to say something. In my broken English, I said, "Only one son, no daughters." Annette answered, "Unfortunately, no daughters. But maybe I can borrow you from your parents." I snickered and covered my face with both my palms. Her kind statement felt reassuring.

Annette then looked at me and said that Jean Pierre spoke some English and so did she, and that between the two of them they should be able to communicate reasonably well with me. She added that in the morning Jean Pierre would take me on a tour of the big hotel to show me where I would be working. When I asked if Jean Pierre knew the hotel well, she said that he did; he cleaned in the summer just like I was scheduled to do, except that he cleaned at the small hotel.

Jean Pierre looked at me and said jokingly, "You are very important. You clean at the big hotel." I said nothing. I just smiled and looked down. To my surprise, we headed to the Allard house. I thought that they would take me to the hotel, to some kind of maids' quarter.

Their house was in the suburbs of Paris, fifteen minutes from the Champs-Élysées, considered the center of Paris, where the two hotels were. When we arrived at the house, I waited to carry my very old, bulky leather suitcase in. Annette asked me not to. Their driver handled my luggage. Stepping into the house, I could see that it was a small mansion with a big entry rotunda and two spiral staircases, one on each side. Naturally, coming from a refugee camp, I was not only impressed; I was overwhelmed. I still wasn't sure if I would be staying at the Allard house for the summer or only for a couple of days, until I got settled.

Annette took me by the hand to a large room. In the bathroom, there were closets on each side. She helped me take off my jacket and hung it in one of the closets. She showed me where to wash my face and where the commode was. After that, Annette called on a female housekeeper and asked her to help me hang my clothes up. The housekeeper spoke very little English, but she managed to communicate through signs and demonstrations without a single hitch. What impressed me most was the fact that my room had its own large bathroom, which was bigger than my bedroom in the refugee camp.

The housekeeper managed to explain things sufficiently until we got to the bidet. I had never seen one before. Despite her endless repeated attempts, I couldn't understand what it was for. As she got frustrated and almost angry, she pulled her dress up, her underwear down, and crouched on top of the bidet, all in my presence. Even then she could tell that I was still confused and embarrassed by the whole thing.

I eventually realized what the bidet was for: to wash oneself after using the toilet. In the process, my lack of familiarity caused my best dress, the one I'd worn on the flight over, to get wet. She helped me dry myself and put my clothes back on, took me to my bedroom, and went to see Annette.

Annette was there in no time to direct the housekeeper what to do. She helped me take off my dress and then she hung it and brought a small fan and proceeded to dry it. The housekeeper asked if I wanted to take a nap, after she pointed to a clock in the room and indicated two hours. I then said my first French word, *Oui*, meaning yes.

Two hours later, Annette knocked on the door and came in, again after I said, "Oui." Annette then demonstrated knocking on the door again and then said, "*Entre*," meaning *enter*, trying to tell me what to say in response to a knock on the door. She told me that I looked rested, and my face looked much younger. She then helped me put on the same dress, after she found out it was my best. She waited for me to get dressed, took me to the bathroom, and helped me comb my hair. By the time we finished, I looked much better than when my mother fixed me up.

Annette took me down to the dining room. She sat at one end of the eight-seater table. She seated me to her right, Jean Pierre sat to her left, and Antoine sat to my right. The chairs were very comfortable, but what attracted my attention most was the plate setup. There were two forks on the left, two knives on the right, and one spoon.

The housekeeper brought a large bowl of cream of asparagus soup first and poured some in my soup dish. I had never heard of asparagus before. I could see that the soup dish sat on top of another dish. I didn't know what the second dish underneath was for. As we started with the soup, I immediately noticed that I was the only one slurping. The soup was different from the lentil or vegetable soups I was used to. I quickly noticed my slurping and adjusted right away. I could hear Annette saying something to Antoine and Jean Pierre. Then she said to me, "You are a quick learner." I figured it was all about the slurping.

After the soup, we were served coq au vin, a most delicious chicken in wine sauce with vegetables. Annette explained to me that they used wine, but the alcohol in the wine had evaporated right away, and the dish had none by the time it was finished. She also said that her coq au vin had no pork. The following day, Friday, they planned to serve couscous for dinner since it was supposedly my kind of food. I told her that I had never heard of couscous (and I didn't want to hear the name again, as it referred to a woman's genitalia). Annette said that they used to eat couscous every Friday in Algeria.

This was the first time I learned that they had lived in Algeria, an Arab country. Jean Pierre excused himself when he saw the expression on my face. He came back with a huge book in his hand that looked like some kind of food encyclopedia. He looked up couscous and found four pages of full description: where it originated, what it meant, and how it was prepared. He looked at his parents and said something I couldn't understand except for two words, *Kabyle* and *Arabe*. He kept reading and tried to pronounce a difficult word, *moghrabiyeh*. After several attempts, he managed to pronounce the word enough for me to understand what he was saying. Then he said, after I nodded my head approvingly, "Tomorrow, moghrabiyeh." I said OK and smiled.

Annette then tried to explain to me that she didn't know, although having lived in Algeria for six years, that couscous was originally a Kabyle dish. I asked her what she meant by *Kabyle*. She said that Kabyle meant Amazigh. I still didn't know what they meant. Jean Pierre ran up again and brought down a huge dictionary. He looked up Kabyle and then wrote down *Kaba'il*. I could then follow. He was referring to the original tribes of North Africa. *Kabyle* turned out to be a corrupt form of the word *Kaba'il*.

Annette apologized and said that she didn't know that the word *couscous* was bad in Arabic. It was used in North Africa because it belonged to the original inhabitants, the Amazigh. I told her that it was strange that some Arab countries would continue to use such a name. We laughed it off.

When I tried to eat the coq au vin with my spoon, Annette stood up, moved behind me, gave me the large fork and the large knife, and started to demonstrate how to use them. At the beginning it felt strange, since I couldn't scoop the sauce with a fork. But in short order, I managed well and started imitating Annette's intricate moves. Antoine noticed what I was doing and was impressed with my arm and mouth movements. He said, "*Bravo, magnifique*" and clapped his hands toward me.

At that point, Annette realized that I needed some social etiquette coaching. She looked at Jean Pierre and told him that I would not start working the following day and that instead she wanted to take me shopping. Jean Pierre accepted with tepid enthusiasm, after he translated what Annette had said. Then he asked if I would be starting the day after. Annette answered that she would let him know the following day.

In the morning, Annette asked me if I cared for some beef sausage, taking into consideration that I didn't eat pork. I told them that I did not eat any meat in the morning and only occasionally had eggs. At eleven we went out and, to my surprise, Annette took me to a Syrian grocery store. She asked me to buy anything that matched my diet in Amman. I bought yogurt spread, white cheese, thyme, fava beans, garbanzo beans, and Arabic bread. Annette was surprised at the limited choices I made. I told her that I saw olive oil, tomatoes, and jam at her house and with those my morning ingredients were complete.

After that, we went to a very fashionable young women's dress shop. There, after consulting with me, Annette bought me three dresses, six slips, six pairs of underwear, and six bras. I hadn't started wearing a bra yet; not because I didn't want to, but because it was not a necessary item and without it my parents could save money. Annette could tell that I was more than happy with our shopping spree. At the very end, she hugged me and kissed me on my forehead. Again, it was so soothing and reassuring.

In the evening, sitting at the dining table, I wore one of my new dresses. Jean Pierre was the first to comment. He told me that I looked beautiful and that his mother had very discriminating taste. I replied that she was great and so loving. When Jean Pierre looked at his mother and father, Annette translated what I had said about her to Antoine. Annette then looked at Jean Pierre and said, "You're lucky. Now you have the sister you've always wanted—and it's perfect, because you're seventeen and she's sixteen."

Jean Pierre didn't seem to like the idea and looked confused. "A sister!" he said. "No, she will be my friend, a very charming and close friend." Annette looked at me and asked, "Would you rather be Jean Pierre's sister or his friend?" I could tell what the mild disagreement was all about. I said, "How about if I will be both a sister and a friend, because some sisters are not too friendly toward their brothers?" Annette looked at me and nodded her head with an expression of admiration. When she translated my answer to Antoine, he said, "A friend is more important than a sister. Sisters and brothers fight a lot."

Jean Pierre looked at his father and said, "Bravo, Papa, I agree." The conversation then moved to the subject of couscous. Annette said, "I'm sorry, but I can't pronounce the name in Arabic. I must stick to the Kabyle name, if you don't mind." I shook my head side to side, indicating that I didn't mind. I then added, "I'll call it moghrabiyeh, and you call it whatever you want. Deal?" Annette, Jean Pierre, and Antoine all agreed, all smiling in good spirits.

Then Antoine started speaking, and Jean Pierre translated. He said that he and Annette were ashamed of what the French did while occupying Algeria. He added that he would take every opportunity to help the Arabs as a way of making up for this abuse. It occurred to me that I might be the beneficiary of some past regretful experience on the part of the Allards. I didn't say anything, as I felt I wasn't informed or mature enough to delve into such a complex subject.

That evening, I lay down in bed and started thinking. I found myself totally surprised but almost enchanted and impressed with my behavior. For one thing, I seemed to pick up on things fast. I had never used a fork and knife together at the same time, yet their use felt almost natural to me. I had never worn a bra before in my life, yet I felt as if my new bra was part of me. Above all, I had never worn soft and skimpy underwear before, yet I didn't feel naked; I felt more feminine, and when I pulled my dress and slip up to look at myself, I was impressed with what I saw.

For the first time, I could see how every item Annette bought me enhanced my look, but even more importantly, they transformed the way I looked at my body. Their purpose was not only to cover my figure and body parts but also to shape my figure and expose the beauty of those parts. This is the way I felt when I looked between my legs. What was in between got projected and softened by the silk-like material, which contoured over it. Suddenly, it took shape, and the reflection of such shape was revealing and suggestive. I was not your average sixteen-year-old. Everything is new to me, even the new look of my body!

I was happy with myself, and most appreciative of the hospitality the Allards had shown me. I didn't quite know how to describe them; they were something I hadn't experienced or considered before. And then there was the unexpected addition of Jean Pierre. As reticent as I was with Annette and Antoine, I felt the opposite with Jean Pierre. He was only slightly more mature than I was and just as vulnerable. He was inclined to make simple mistakes. His mistakes would mix with mine, and the mix would create an atmosphere of informality. Those were mere initial impressions; I knew there was only so much I could know in a matter of two days. I knew I needed more time to deepen my impressions into actual conclusions.

Chapter 4

In the morning, Annette accompanied me and Jean Pierre to the hotel. It was large, in a nineteenth-century beaux arts style. The doorman was impeccably dressed and fully aware of what was happening in the street. He immediately noticed us and tipped his hat, recognizing Annette and Jean Pierre, as he swung the door open for us. He tipped his hat again as he called me *mademoiselle*. After we climbed the six stairs, we entered a glorious hall with four bellboys ready to handle luggage and direct guests to the registration desk. There were three desk clerks and two concierges. I surveyed the area all around me and up and down to savor the motif and the panoramic view of the rooms overlooking the main hallway.

As she dropped us off, Annette told me that she went over my training for the day with Jean Pierre and that she would go over the rest of the training program with him, day by day. She kissed me on both cheeks, straightened my hair over my head, and said *"au revoir."*

Jean Pierre opened a side door for me and guided me to the concierge desk, where he was greeted deferentially. Jean Pierre asked the concierge for Najiba. She was waiting for us on the second floor. On the way there, Jean Pierre explained that Najiba was Moroccan and that he would tell her how to train me. He said that it would be easier because Najiba spoke Arabic, instead of he and I trying to communicate in broken English.

I met Najiba and introduced myself. I could barely understand her when she asked, "Is this an Arab name?" When I said yes, she gave me a surprised look. She tried to explain things to me, but I could only understand a few words. I looked at Jean Pierre and told him that I couldn't understand her properly and that she spoke in her local dialect, which was far removed from mine. When he asked if Najiba could understand me, I told him that she could understand me better than I could understand her, but not entirely. He paused and then told me that the only thing Najiba was able to teach me that he couldn't was mopping the floor, and therefore he'd do the training himself and include Najiba at the very end. I smiled and nodded my head to clearly let him know that I preferred it that way.

The first thing he did was give me a uniform. It was tailored and cute: The blouse was striped in white and marine blue, the skirt was solid blue, and the apron was also striped in white and blue, but with much thinner stripes than the blouse. He knocked on the door of the cleaning staff room. When we went in, he showed me where to hang my clothes and where to change. When I finished changing into my uniform, he came back and looked at me. I could see it in his eyes; he was impressed with how I looked.

He showed me how to knock on the guest room doors and what to say. When I stumbled pronouncing some of the words, he told me not to worry about it and that he would go over it again in the evening, at home, as long as I needed it. When he said that, I thought that this meant I'd probably be living with the Allards instead of in the maids' quarter of the hotel.

That evening, when Jean Pierre and I went back to the house together, he insisted that I keep my uniform on. When we got there, he called his mother. When she looked at me, she raised both arms and said, "*Mon dieu, quelle beauté*," meaning "My god, what a beauty." Antoine followed Annette and when he saw me, he had a similar reaction. "You are magnificent; you look so sophisticated."

While Jean Pierre had an air of accomplishment all over his face, Annette walked up to my room and asked me to shower, change, and then come down for a drink. When I came down, Annette asked if I wanted a beer or a glass of wine. I told her that I did not drink alcohol. "Sure," she said, but then I said, "Why not, I am in France; I will take white wine." She then said that I could have half a glass. I didn't have any idea how wine tasted. After I took my first two sips, all that I could tell was that wine had a strange taste. Yet I enjoyed it, since the experience felt daring and adventurous.

When Antoine saw me drinking, he said that it was OK since the Arabs were the ones who had introduced alcohol to the West. I was very skeptical about his statement. Then he explained to me that the Arabs used to distill mascara, and since *mascara* meant *alcohol* in Arabic, the crusaders thought that alcohol meant distilling. Upon their return to Europe, they began distilling and called it *alcohol*, from which alcoholic drinks came to be known. I understood what Antoine was saying in general, but the details were confusing.

Over the weekend, Annette took me again to buy blouses and skirts, some with a similar pattern to my uniform. She told me I looked beautiful in that combination. From that point on, it was kind of a pastime for Annette to take me shopping over the weekend and try to fit me with all kinds of clothes. After she threw away all the clothes I brought along, I ended up with eight dresses and skirts and a dozen blouses.

Jean Pierre was doing a marvelous job teaching me all kinds of French words and sentences. After he finished training me, I always looked forward to getting together with him after work, since he worked at the small hotel during the day. Time was passing so quickly. I must confess, I was having an exalting out-of-body experience, living in a house with a driver and housekeeper and being cared for in a most loving way.

By the fifth week, my attitude had changed, and my new life began to feel natural and almost tailor-made for me. I decided to be circumspect when sharing my experience with my parents. It was too good to be true and way too luxurious in comparison to their style of living. Above all, I started thinking of myself as a guest of the Allards, rather than a cleaning person at a hotel. I felt they were thinking of me the same way.

One evening, as Jean Pierre was teaching me French, with the two of us sitting on my bed against the wall, I asked him if he could read to me poems by de Lamartine. He was surprised I had heard of de Lamartine. I reminded him that my father was a French language teacher. He then asked if I knew any other French authors. I told him that I'd read in Arabic about the life and loves of Alexandre Dumas. When he asked me what I knew about Dumas, I told him that I'd read about his adventures and, best of all, about his romances with over forty women.

Jean Pierre continued to probe. At first, I said that since I hadn't actually read his novels and only read about him, all in Arabic, maybe what I'd read wasn't true. "OK, before I read to you some of de Lamartine's poems, you need to describe to me what the Arabic book said about Dumas," Jean Pierre said. I told him that the book I'd read described Dumas as a great lover and that he knew how to treat his lovers.

Jean Pierre kept asking for more specifics. When I told him that Dumas was very successful with women and managed to seduce them by soothing their feelings before he made love to them, Jean Pierre then asked what specifically Dumas did to soothe his lovers' feelings and insisted that I describe what I'd read in detail. I remembered one act clearly. It described Dumas massaging the thighs of his lovers up and down repeatedly and gently before he made love.

I shared the description of the massage with Jean Pierre. He asked what happened next. I said, "You know" and stopped. He said, "No, I don't know, tell me."

"You know, they made love afterward," I said. He then looked at me and asked, "Have you ever made love?" I got off the bed and said, "No, of course not. Have you made love yourself, Jean Pierre?"

"To be honest, yes, three times," he replied.

I paused for a short while looking at him, not knowing what to say, but then I gave him a disgusted look and asked, "And how many got pregnant?"

"What do you mean?" he asked. "I'm careful, and they are careful. We know when to make love." "When?" I asked. He told me that there was a specific time every month when a women couldn't get pregnant.

While I knew in general about this, I didn't know the specifics. "When is that?" I asked.

"To be on the safe side, it's between six days and eleven days after a woman gets her period," he explained. "I'm very careful," he added.

To change the subject, I said, "Do you want to read me poems from de Lamartine?" He looked at my skirt and said, "I will after I fix the loose hem of your skirt."

I looked down at my skirt suspiciously and saw that he was right: The hem of my skirt was loose halfway around. He excused himself and returned with a needle and thread. After asking if I didn't mind, he proceeded to stitch the hem while he was sitting down at the edge of the bed. I was standing up, his face facing my thighs.

He was doing a good job until the needle got loose, thrusting into my left thigh. Jean Pierre raised my skirt almost six inches up and tried to wipe the blood off my thigh. He took my hand and placed my finger on the cut. He then got up and fetched a bandage. After he wrapped the bandage around my thigh, he lowered my skirt and said, "You have very beautiful legs. They look like off-white marble and are so smooth." I said nothing; I didn't know what to say.

The cut was very minor, yet he insisted on helping me by sitting me down on the bed and settling my back against the headboard, while he sat next to me. He then read to me two poems of de Lamartine, one of which was "The Lake." He took his time translating every line. When he finished reading that poem, he said some of it applied to him. When I asked what part, he said that he'd tell me later. It was getting late; Jean Pierre said that I needed to rest since the following day the hotel had a banquet for three hundred guests.

Before he left, he asked me if he could kiss me good night on my cheek. I said, "On my cheek, yes."

I'd found it so easy to let Jean Pierre kiss me on my cheek—something that could never have happened in Amman. Yet I wasn't apprehensive in the least. I just liked it and thought nothing of it. I was picking up the French tempo with utmost ease, mostly discarding the perimeters that applied back in the refugee camp. I was getting used to the food, the comfort of a luxurious home, and the flowing kindness of my hosts, as if they were family.

I wondered whether Jean Pierre was starting to develop feelings for me. I wasn't sure—so far so good, but surely his pressing me with questions about Dumas seemed like a signal that he was measuring his emotions toward me. I wondered if it was my improved looks and posture that was making him change or if he harbored the same emotions for me as he did for any other acceptable girl. I didn't have an answer to this. Thinking about his attitude also made me examine my own.

After I brushed my teeth, washed my face, and brushed my hair, I went to bed in an ethereal mood. I felt like congratulating myself. I hadn't known that I had it in me to adapt to French culture so easily and to please the Allards to the degree I seemed to be doing. Not only that, but the service manager at the hotel was satisfied with my performance. He told Antoine that, unlike most of his cleaning staff, I didn't waste time yapping or socializing. He'd already asked Antoine to bring me back the following summer. With difficulty, I got this information from Najiba, who was sleeping with the service manager. Their relationship had started when he engaged her to clean his bachelor apartment once a week.

The rest of the summer continued with the same pleasant pattern. Annette started calling me "Yara, my love," and Antoine referred to me as his beautiful butterfly. Ten weeks into my visit, I surprised Antoine by talking to him in French, hesitantly at first, but using the right words and expressions. I suddenly felt free to interrupt my conversation to describe the word I was looking for, and most of the time whoever was listening to me would direct me.

Jean Pierre kept giving me a kiss on my cheek every evening as he said goodnight. During my eleventh week, he told me he wanted to read to me a stanza from "The Lake" that applied to him. I said, "Grand," in French. He asked me to stand up and face him just as I had when he fixed the hem of my skirt. He was looking straight at my thighs. He told me he was reading to me since I was leaving the following week and that what he planned to read related to him and me.

> *Let's love, then! Love, and feel while we can*
> *The moment on its run.*
> *There is no shore of Time, no port of Man.*
> *It flows, and we go on.*

I stopped and said nothing because I understood then what he was alluding to. When I asked him if de Lamartine meant to express what he was expressing, he said, "I don't care what de Lamartine wanted to express as long as you understand what *I* am expressing." I slowly dragged my feet a few inches toward him and stopped between his legs, with him sitting at the edge of the bed and his feet on the floor. He raised my skirt and put his right palm onto my left thigh. He then put his left palm onto my right thigh and started massaging it, just like I'd described the way Dumas must have done it.

It took him a few minutes before he moved his right hand to the center. I removed his hand and put it back on my thigh. He tried once more, also unsuccessfully. He kept massaging my thighs and then my buttocks for another twenty minutes. Both of us were getting aroused. I then pushed him down onto the bed and lay down next to him.

He knew I wasn't going to let him go all the way. He raised himself up, took my right hand, and slowly and carefully placed it on my genitalia, over my silk-like panties. He then helped me with the motion of masturbating. When he removed his hand, he stood up, nodded his head for me to continue, and walked slowly out of the room. I continued for ten more minutes before I reached my first climax, courtesy of Jean Pierre's coaching. I hadn't known that it could be that enjoyable.

The evening before leaving for Amman, I went with the Allards to a fish restaurant. It was the best restaurant I had ever been to—beyond my wildest imagination. Antoine took me by my hand to choose three kinds of fish out of fifty different choices, all delivered fresh to the restaurant every four hours, sixteen hours a day. The evening was superlative. Annette told me several times about how much she was going to miss me. Then Antoine said, "We want you to come back next year and stay with us all summer. Tell your father that your salary will be twice as much."

After hearing all this, and while Jean Pierre was the one saying nothing and showing a sense of loss, I uncharacteristically grabbed Annette's face and kissed her four times, just like my father used to kiss me. I immediately started crying. Jean Pierre's eyes were getting wet before he got up and moved outside, away from the fancy tent of the restaurant. It was Antoine who managed to keep things in check. He kissed Annette first and then he got up and gave me a kiss on my cheek. He then proceeded to bring Jean Pierre back.

I told them at dinner that I was going to leave most of my clothes at the house for next year. Annette shook her head and said, "Impossible." I explained to them that wearing so many fancy dresses in the refugee camp wouldn't feel right. There would be gossip and the speculation that I had been doing something else in France. I explained that all I needed were two dark dresses and my uniform. I could wear the dresses for weddings and funerals, and I could show off my uniform to let everyone know that I was a cleaning person at a very fancy hotel.

Later that evening, Jean Pierre tiptoed to my room and found me daydreaming in bed. The moment he entered the room, I grabbed his right hand, placed it on top of my right hand, and had him push my hand into giving myself a climax. Little did I know that my pleasure was his frustration. I imagined later that he must have gone to his room and masturbated to relieve himself.

Annette insisted on going out to the airport with me alone. Both Antoine and Jean Pierre intended to go too, but didn't want to disagree with Annette. The two gave me a very warm and cuddly hug.

"Make sure that I see you next year," Jean Pierre whispered in my ear. Antoine said, "Paris suits you. You are now a more beautiful and vibrant young woman. By the time you come back you will be even lovelier."

On the way to the airport, Annette asked me indirectly if I'd packed the fancy panties. "Yes," I said. Neither my father nor anybody else would be able to see what I was wearing under my dresses. Annette continued by saying that, now that she knew me, she had ideas for the following year. "Don't tell your father," she said. "We're going to pretend that next year you will be working at the hotel, too. My plan is for you to be tutored in French three hours a day, and then you and I will be socializing all the time. I will also help you with your French—not Jean Pierre. He needs to concentrate on passing his baccalaureate exam."

I didn't know what to think about this. I was getting to like Jean

Pierre a lot, not only for teaching me French, but for connecting me with my own body. No, I wasn't in love with him, but I was enchanted with his gentle approach and care. He never forced himself on me, although he could have easily done so.

Annette hugged me goodbye at the airport and kissed me on both cheeks, cuddling my head over her shoulder. I could see that she was sad I was leaving. I told her to share with Jean Pierre and Antoine that my three-month stay was the best thing that had ever happened to me, that I had never expected to be treated so generously and so warmly by anyone, and that they were the finest family I had ever met.

"You brought out the best in us, the three of us," she said. "I hope we did the same." She let go as she teared up, and then she turned around and walked away without looking back. I kept looking at her and started crying quietly.

Chapter 5

I was met at the airport by my father and mother and also, surprisingly, Jean Garnier, the French attaché. Garnier had been receiving glowing reports from Annette, which were relayed to my parents. I could see in their faces that they were pleasantly anxious to welcome me home. After my parents kissed me, Garnier gave me two soft kisses on my cheeks. He said, "Annette could not stop talking about you. She feels years younger since your visit." My father looked me in the eye and said, "You are a young woman now, and you have made me and your mother proud."

The combination of the three is what I needed then. I wanted to feel the warmth of my parents but didn't want to disconnect with France. After I hugged my parents, with my mother kissing me around ten times and holding onto me for half a minute, Garnier gave me a hug. It reminded me that while I belonged to Palestine and my parents, I was still connected to France. It felt liberating. Everything I had been told about the French seemed to be wrong. They were not pompous and arrogant toward foreigners. Garnier and the Allards could not have been sweeter.

Garnier took over the conversation and asked how I had enjoyed Paris. I told him that I hadn't been to any other major city but that

Paris was heaven. I added that the Allards were the most beautiful people I had ever met, and since my father had never connected with his half-brother, I considered them to be more like my uncle and aunt.

Garnier then asked about their son, totally unexpectedly. I paused before I collected my thoughts and said, "He was always with his friends on his scooter. I barely saw him. I always had dinner with Annette and Antoine; he never showed up for dinner." I emphasized this so as not to cause my father and mother to have any suspicions about a possible relationship between me and Jean Pierre. Garnier noticed nothing. He was pleased that I was so thrilled about my trip.

My mother then commented on my dress—that it was very beautiful and fashionable. I lied again by telling her that Annette bought me two dresses just before my trip back to Amman. My father looked at me and said, "Why are you are referring to the Allards by their first names? You should stick to calling them Mr. and Mrs. Allard." I told him that their son called them by their first names and that they had asked me to do the same. They claimed it was the way it was done in "the new France"; they'd picked up the habit from some of the American tourists at their hotels. Garnier said, "If they want to be called by their first names, then you cannot go against their own wishes. I am sure that Yara wanted to call them by Mr. and Mrs., but they must have stopped her." I nodded my head.

As I started my final year of high school, I had no regrets. I was anxiously waiting to return to France the following summer. I knew I had a major challenge: what to do about college. Despite the additional monthly $100 from the French embassy, my father couldn't afford sending me to college. He'd need another $200 per month.

My plan was to stick to my studies and try to maintain my A average, both at my school and when I took my government exam. Then I'd work in Paris, continuing to learn French until I was fluent, whether I made it to college or not.

Fortunately, everything fell into place. Antoine wrote to my father and told him that they wanted me to work at the hotel the following summer for twice the pay. My father and mother were excited and said yes right away. Their approval was a heavy load off my shoulders. I isolated myself further to study for my exams. My mother even asked me to take it easy. My father asked the same and then suggested that he and I study French together. In a matter of three months, my father managed to elevate my French.

I reconnected with my friend Mira, and I suggested that we read *Lady Chatterley's Lover* together. She bought the book without letting her father know. We read it in Arabic. Mira was curious what my specific interest was in such a book. I brushed its importance aside by saying, "It's a classic, and the two of us should read books like this, about sex and art, before we read other books." Mira agreed with me. It was a glorious read. Between this book and my recollections of Jean Pierre trying to seduce me, I was daydreaming for a couple of hours each evening before going to sleep.

I badly wanted to enjoy myself sexually, but I couldn't since I was sharing the same bedroom with Nader, my brother. He was only eleven. I went to my mother and told her that I was getting embarrassed with Nader in the same room. When she asked what had changed, I told her that my period was getting more intense and that sometimes I couldn't help it: I would get blood on my clothes, and I didn't want Nader to see that. My mother agreed. After she talked to my father, he bought a used folding bed and had Nader start sleeping in the living room. He didn't care. On the contrary, he preferred it that way, for it was easier for him to sneak out to play with his friends.

I started taking liberties. I got into masturbating two or three times a week. It felt so good. All the time, I would imagine Jean Pierre caressing me. I had no crush on anybody else. I was careful not to show my fancy and sexy panties to my mother. One day she came into the bedroom and caught me in them. "What are you doing, wearing this see-through underwear? I can see everything," she said. "Aren't you ashamed of yourself?" I'd fortunately prepared for that moment. I told her that the three pieces of underwear I had taken to France absorbed too much blood and ended up messing up the Allards' laundry. Instead, the stains on these could be washed with ease. I told her that the Allards threw out my old underwear. My mother was convinced but told me not to let my father see my fancy underwear.

After that, whenever my mother noticed me washing my underwear when my father wasn't around, she assumed I was doing so before his return. I was really doing it to conceal their stained condition from my mother.

I was receiving monthly letters from Jean Pierre and Annette, and her fourth letter included an inquiry about my plans for college. I answered with a long letter. I told her that my dream was to study human physiology in the United States, but, realistically, I could settle for the same in Jordan or in France, if possible. I was hoping to receive an answer about my college choices in France, but none came. Her letters continued to cover her plans for teaching me French and the program for our social activities together, and nothing else.

I was very disappointed after her inquiry aroused my expectations. In the meantime, my studies were going exceedingly well, and with the help of my father, my French was improving all the time. I passed my government exam with flying colors. My father was beside himself. I scored eighth "in the Kingdom," as Jordan was referred to—way up in the first percentile. The ministry of education contacted me and offered me a scholarship. I immediately wrote to Annette to tell her that my going to college was no longer a problem.

I was surprised to have Garnier visit us unannounced. He told my father and me that Annette had called him right away upon receiving the news about my Jordanian scholarship to say that she had managed to get me a full scholarship to the United States, as a result of scoring easily in the top 2 percent on the Jordanian government high school exam. My father looked at me to gauge whether I knew about this. My facial expressions reflected the fact that I did not. He told Garnier that I was in the top one tenth of 1 percent but that he didn't want me to go to the United States. Garnier said that he didn't know the details of the American scholarship but that it covered room, board, books, and $80 monthly in pocket money.

My father went silent. He wasn't expecting any other offer than the one from the Ministry of Education. He asked Garnier if he could give us time to think about it. Garnier said that we should think about it carefully but let him know soon, and that he would tell Annette to wait for his answer. Within a week, my father called Garnier and asked if the decision could wait until I visited the Allards. Annette informed Garnier that it could.

Annette sent me my ticket, and I was off to Paris within two weeks. Again, I was met by all three of them. I was wearing the same dress I'd worn when I had returned to Amman. My reception was more than warm; I felt like a long-lost daughter. While Annette went to the bathroom, Jean Pierre held my hand and took me aside to convince me not to go to the United States. I might be able to study at the Sorbonne in Paris, he told me. I replied that my French was still poor. He tried to convince me that by the end of the summer it would not be. I didn't know what to say, but I knew I wasn't ready to study at the university level in French.

As soon as I showered, I went to see Annette. She was holding two new dresses and asked me to choose one. As I was putting on the new dress, Annette pointed to my bosom and said, "They got bigger. Be careful. I need to buy you larger bras." I was embarrassed to say anything, but I did look at them and happened to agree with her. They had become round, solid, and sexy.

At dinner that evening, the subject of college came up right away. Jean Pierre immediately brought up my attending the Sorbonne. Annette said that the Sorbonne was fine, but it didn't provide anything other than free tuition. Jean Pierre said that I could live with them. Annette said that I deserved to accomplish things on my own, according to my own preferences, and while they were ready and able to put me through college, it was better for me not to be defined by her and Antoine but by my own experiences and choices. Antoine agreed and said, "This will also give us the opportunity to visit Yara in the United States." The argument was settled as far as the Allards were concerned: two to one.

The give-and-take of the evening managed to convince me that my future education pointed to the United States. Annette then proceeded to explain the details of my scholarship. It was secured by the US cultural attaché in Paris. He did it as a favor to Antoine, since Antoine always accommodated the needs of the American embassy by providing rooms and halls on short notice at his five-star boutique hotels.

The scholarship came from Berea College, in Kentucky. It was known to be a top college, catering exclusively to students with financial needs. Many of its students continued their education at top universities like Harvard, Yale, and Princeton. Berea had a history of fighting to educate students with different ethnic backgrounds and was known to have challenged some of the nineteenth-century Southern states' restrictions on the education of Black students. The American cultural attaché managed to augment Berea's scholarship with another one from the Quaker church.

The following evening, I spoke briefly to all three, with a low but firm voice. I told them that I had decided to go to America. Jean Pierre got mad and left the table. I asked Annette to call Garnier to let my father know. Garnier relayed the message, and my father sent back an answer saying that although it wasn't his choice, he respected my decision and wished me success. Jean Pierre made himself scarce for two days. During dinner on the third day, I said that I understood that Jean Pierre wanted the best for me and that he thought that the Sorbonne was it. "Now that things are settled, I'll let you know after I get there if Berea was the right choice," I explained.

After dinner, I waited for Annette and Antoine to go to bed. I tiptoed to Jean Pierre's room. He was all agitated in bed, barely asleep. I slipped myself under the same cover, grabbed his face, and gave him a kiss on his lips. I told him that today was the seventh day. He knew what I meant. He was very surprised; he looked at me and started breathing heavily. He pulled up my night dress and took it off. He could see right away my firm and ripe breasts, almost twice the size they were the year before. He grabbed one and sucked on it slowly for almost five minutes.

I was ready and receptive. I slipped my panties off, nodding my head in approval, and he penetrated me after putting a towel in my mouth so that I wouldn't make a loud sound from the pain of losing my virginity. I made a muffled one, and then it was fine. We made love four times. I'd never felt so satisfied and relaxed. We went to sleep in each other's arms. At around five in the morning, Jean Pierre woke me up in a hurry so that the housekeeper wouldn't catch us together. He managed to replace the bloody sheets with clean ones, and the housekeeper didn't notice anything different.

Quietly, I had made an important decision: I would go to the States without first going back to Amman. Before I left, and almost a month after we had had sex for the first time, Jean Pierre asked Annette if he could take me for three days and nights on a group outing. He told Annette that there would be around eighteen girls and ten boys, and that I would sleep in a big tent with the girls. He explained that because I was in the company of adults all the time, my French was still too formal. If I mingled with a younger crowd, I'd pick up young people's lingo. Annette was convinced. When I got there, there were only ten small tents, and including me, there were ten boys and ten girls.

For three nights, Jean Pierre and I slept in the same tent and made love until he was exhausted. I was satisfied and elated every time.

Again, it was a glorious summer. Annette couldn't find enough clothes to buy me. I left Paris with three overweight cases, which cost Annette and Antoine a bundle to ship. My French was much better, and I was practically fluent.

Annette organized the last three days to the minute, making sure we had a full ten-hour schedule each day. She didn't want to stay idle and use the time to dwell on the fact that I was leaving. After my last night in Paris—my last time making love with Jean Pierre—he somehow didn't wake up on time. I was already dressed to go down to breakfast. Annette went up to see Jean Pierre. There were obvious signs of our lovemaking, and it must have been a big surprise to her. It couldn't have been anybody else but me; the housekeeper was older than Annette. Annette called me, ostensibly to help her wake up Jean Pierre. I could tell that she wanted to let me know that she knew.

At the breakfast table, she was smiling but slightly pensive. She must have been wondering how long the relationship had been going on and if we'd taken the proper precautions. At the airport, Annette hugged me as tears rolled down her cheeks. I hugged her back, crying too. I don't know how I summoned the courage, but I managed to whisper to her, "It's all right, don't worry. Jean Pierre is a fine gentleman."

Annette hugged me again, kissed me on my forehead, and said, "You are a fine and beautiful young lady. I am so happy you have become part of our lives." She let go and wrapped one arm around Jean Pierre and another around Antoine. They turned around and left without looking back, per Annette's directions.

Chapter 6

It took me two days to get to Berea College, after flying first to New York and then to Louisville. In Louisville, a Berea counselor, a male student from Honduras, met me and another student from South Korea. When I asked the counselor how long he had been working at Berea, he answered that he was a senior student, and his job was part of the Berea model where students had to work at the college in addition to their studies. He reminded me that I needed to take care of this aspect during my registration.

The Honduran student immediately struck up a conversation with me. He was pleasantly natural and forward. He started by asking my name and told me his: Marco. When I told him that I was Palestinian, he told me that he knew several Palestinians in Honduras. At first I thought he was making that up just to talk to me, but later I found out that there were around 1,500 Palestinians in Honduras at the time. The Korean student said nothing other than hello and goodbye. My first impression of Kentucky, especially the Berea campus, was different from how I imagined it. The American attaché in Paris, who had graduated from Stanford University, did not speak highly of Kentucky. According to Annette, he had referred to it as one of the underdeveloped parts of the country. The greenery was all around, lush and visually pleasing.

After the airport, we had a three-hour bus ride to campus. Just as we arrived, Marco said that he liked my name and that his name was likewise simple, but different. He told me that he was planning to study mostly physics and math, and I told him I was planning to major in biology and minor in French. When he asked me why I wanted to study French, I explained that my father was a French teacher. As far as biology, I planned to become a teacher or even a professor of human physiology, if I was lucky enough to go to graduate school.

Stepping off the bus, I was impressed by the expanse of the campus and the American colonial design of the buildings. In the package I'd received from the American cultural attaché' in Paris, there were several brochures showing the charm of the campus, but looking at it in person was even more impressive.

I was guided to my room in one of the girls' dorms. To my disappointment, I found out that I had been assigned a roommate, who was already settled. Her name was Julie Anne Baxter. She was from the state of West Virginia and, just like me, starting her freshman year. She spoke to me in her mild West Virginia dialect while lying in bed. She looked well-kept, slim, tall, and slightly pale. After having been educated in fashion by Annette, I could tell that Julie Anne dressed in simple but well-coordinated clothes.

I could understand her well. When it came time for me to talk, I was afraid she might not understand my heavily accented English. My speech was slow and hesitant. She looked me in the eyes and said, "Don't worry. I can understand every word you say, just say them without hesitating. You speak good English." I just smiled and said nothing.

She stood up to look at me closely, as if she were considering me for a dance or a play. "Maybe you and I will double-date," she said. "I just broke up with my boyfriend in West Virginia. He was a hillbilly and tried to convince me not to go to college. I wasn't going to do that. I am the second to go to college in my extended family."

I told her that I had two cousins on my mother's side who had gone to university; one was an electrical engineer, and the other was an economist. I then told her that I had a half uncle on my father's side, but I didn't know him or his children. I told her that I knew he was dead.

She went back to asking me about double-dating. When I told her that I didn't understand what she meant, she explained it to me. She added, "But we don't have to end the evening in the same room, of course! You'll do your thing in one room, and I'll do mine in another." When I asked her what thing she was referring to, she said, "Don't pretend you don't know! The international language. You don't have to be an American to get it."

I still couldn't follow what she was talking about. Julie Anne said, "The international language! Sex! We can't have sex in the same room." I looked at her and said nothing. She continued, "I know you're better looking and taller than me, but I know how to attract them. Don't worry about me."

By the time she had finished her talk about dating and sex, I had decided that I didn't want anything to do with her, besides being roommates. But slowly, her attitude grew on me; she volunteered to help me anytime she could, and she went out of her way to introduce me to the American way of life. Once, she took me to a special pie bakery seven miles from Berea that had been in business for more than fifty years—her aunt had told her about it from when she had been a student at Berea twenty-five years earlier. Julie Anne explained about pies, going through eleven different kinds, including pecan and mincemeat.

Two weeks into the semester, Julie Anne said that she'd run into two handsome brothers, one a sophomore and the other a freshman, who preferred double dating. "I told them we'd be interested in going out this weekend—provided you approve. Take a peek at the taller one." I said sarcastically that I'd like to look at the taller one, but I wouldn't accept being in separate rooms.

"You mean you want us to see each other while we're doing it?" Julie Anne asked.

"Sure, we can look at each other all the time while we're talking and joking," I replied half sarcastically.

Julie Anne got mad. "I'm not going on a date to talk and joke." I said, "OK, then you date both brothers." Julie Anne got even madder, lay in her bed, and turned her face toward the wall.

We barely talked for two days. As we were studying, the phone rang and was picked up by Julie Anne. I could hear her saying "Marco who?" I realized it was Marco from Honduras. While I hadn't thought I would hear from him again, I told Julie Anne that the call was for me.

Marco invited me for dinner on Friday, to a Mexican restaurant. I'd never even heard of Mexican food. I accepted the invitation, to spite Julie Anne more than anything else. Marco was a gentleman, mild and circumspect. All he talked about was the Palestinian-owned haberdashery in his Honduran village. We spent two and a half hours together. When I got back, Julie Anne was sulking. She said nothing. I offered her my boxed food. To my surprise, she took it. She hadn't made it to the cafeteria on time, feeling sorry for herself.

I took the opportunity to speak to her. "You have to ask me first before you make any plans," I said. To my surprise, Julie Anne not only agreed to accommodate my request, but she also apologized for being presumptuous. She asked me about Marco. I told her gently that I was a private person and that she didn't need to tell me anything about her dates, and I didn't need to tell her about mine. She said that was the way she related with her cousins. They told each other everything after each date. Having discussed the same subject with the Allards, I said, "Remember, I am not your cousin. I am your roommate."

After that, Julie Anne became very deferential to me. By the end of the semester, she'd gotten even more so, especially when she found out that I scored straight As in all five courses. She had three Bs and two Cs. I had also gone on three dates with Marco, all of them ending uneventfully. While Marco behaved most properly, he stopped asking me out. I recalled then that he paid for all three dinners. I told myself that I wanted to invite him out for dinner at least once, as a way to pay him back.

One weekend, I got on the bus and headed for Richmond, thirteen miles away. It was a small city more than twice the size of Berea. There I ran into the owner of a supermarket who happened to be of Lebanese origin. His name was George. When he realized I was Palestinian, he extended a dinner invitation to his home. He told me that it was no bother and that he would drive me back to Berea after we visited with his wife, Leila. He told me that she was very lonely. He had been born in Kentucky, but she was born in Lebanon and hadn't yet acclimated to the social scene in Kentucky. She later called me and promised to cook up a storm for me, anything I was craving. I apologized and told her that I had promised my roommate that I'd have dinner with her and two other students at the college cafeteria but that I would cherish a rain check.

Suddenly, my paying back Marco came to mind. I asked her if she minded if I brought a friend along. She welcomed the idea. I called Marco and told him about Leila and her husband, and that if he were available, he and I could have dinner at their home that coming Friday. Marco accepted readily, as he was fond of Arabic food, having been invited to dinner by a Palestinian high school friend in Honduras many times.

The evening with Leila and George was wonderful. On top of ten appetizer dishes and three main dishes, Leila gave each of us an assortment of samples, including dessert. Marco was impressed. I brought some back to share with Julie Anne, who loved the food. I was warming up to Marco and Julie Anne by then. Although she was a country girl, Julie Anne was very sweet and meant well. I was a refugee camp girl but had been transformed by two summers in France. As for Marco, I was impressed by his gentlemanly behavior. He was so deferential and so smart. He taught me so much about Latin America, its politics, and its economic conditions. In many ways, it sounded like he was describing the Middle East.

I was carrying a full load of classes at Berea and working twelve hours a week at the information office, preparing folders for the board of trustees of the different activities at the college. One day, out of nowhere, there was someone hanging over my shoulder. He was a rugged-looking Black man, well-groomed and smartly dressed. I stood up to face him, looking at his round face and brown eyes. He was taller than I was.

He said that I wasn't filing all that needed to be included in the folders. He introduced himself as Moens Thomasson and told me that he had done this before in high school and that he could show me how to do it properly.

When I asked what was missing, he couldn't come up with anything. I was slightly miffed at his criticism and also at his attitude. Two days later, he was there again, asking if I was free over the weekend for dinner. I immediately said no. There was another reason I said no, besides his arrogant attitude: he was a Black American, and I'd never had any contact with one up to that point. Growing up, our camp didn't have a single black-skinned Arab, and the first time I'd ever seen a Black person at all was in Paris. Likewise, I had never seen an Asian person until I visited Paris. Although 15 percent of the students at Berea were Black, I decided that I wasn't interested in venturing out of my comfort zone.

Moens tried several times, and each time I turned him down. It was getting embarrassing. His fourth invitation was to a college dance, to which I answered that I was going but that I had another date. But I made a mistake in telling him that. My plan entailed going with Julie Anne and for the two of us to have fun dancing the night away without any attachment. I was eager to try the dances Jean Pierre had taught me. I told Julie Anne about my mistake with Moens and let her know that I had to have a date to go to the dance, or I'd have to cancel my plans for going altogether.

I called Marco and asked him to go to the dance. He was more than happy to be my date. We hadn't even kissed. I masturbated when Julie Anne was out of town. Jean Pierre was always my sexual prop, although I wasn't in love with him.

At the dance, Marco got to drinking heavily. Sometimes he laid his head on my shoulder, and suddenly he started kissing me on my neck. By then I'd had one glass of wine. I was in the mood that evening, and I was tired of waiting for Julie Anne to be out of town, so I filled my glass with more wine and chugged it down. In no time, I felt less inhibited.

I helped Marco leave the dance floor to walk into the wooded area of the campus. He kept kissing me on my neck. I backed myself against a solid white oak tree and directed his hand to massage me. He tried to unzip his slacks. I zipped them back up. Once again, I directed his hand. He got the message and before long he helped me reach a climax. He then tried to have me give him a blow job. It didn't appeal to me. Instead, I massaged his penis. I thought this made us even.

Later that night, I had to think about what had happened. I knew that giving Marco or anybody else a blow job didn't appeal to me, but why not have sex with him, just like with Jean Pierre, on a few occasions? My rationalization was that Jean Pierre was very gentle and considerate, and my relationship with him had not been this casual.

Annette and I were in constant communication, at the rate of one letter exchanged a month. At the end of the first year, she wrote to ask if Berea was turning out to be the ideal choice. My answer to her was a resounding yes. I sent her a copy of my grades: ten courses with a straight-A average. Four weeks later, she sent me a thousand-dollar check, writing that it was for the first year and that she and Antoine thereafter would be sending me a hundred dollars a month. That was significant money, on top of the eighty-dollar pocket money I was already receiving courtesy of the efforts of the cultural attaché in Paris.

I told Julie Anne that Annette, whom I introduced as my aunt in Paris, was helping out and that her money would allow me to patronize nicer restaurants. I volunteered to pay a higher share of the bill if she came with me. Julie Anne welcomed the arrangement and was appreciative. I wanted her to partially experience something of what I had experienced in Paris, eating at fancy restaurants. Julie Anne had described how she used to eat peanut butter and jam for three days straight. Of course, in my case, I'd eaten only yogurt spread for several days at a time while growing up in the refugee camp. Now, I had the false feeling that I'd grown up eating what I'd shared with the Allards in Paris.

It was at a continental restaurant in Richmond where I met Bernard. He was another Frenchman, working in Richmond as a sommelier. I ordered a bottle of an unfamiliar bottle of Gevrey-Chambertin. Burgundy from Gevrey-Chambertin was the Allards' favorite wine. Bernard suggested a different one: "Much better and for four dollars less," he explained. Julie Anne and I drank the whole bottle. It was velvety smooth and balanced, made from the grapes of old vines.

When we finished dinner, I thanked Bernard for his recommendation, in French. He answered that he had a superior Gevrey-Chambertin at home that he would like to share with me. I said that I'd love to sample the wine but that restaurants in Kentucky didn't permit customers to bring their own. He figured right away what I was trying to relay to him, not wanting to visit him at home, and said that he knew a top-notch restaurant that made exceptions in his case. I accepted this arrangement, and we agreed that I'd call him.

I called him two weeks later, minutes before the restaurant where he worked opened. I asked him to tell me more about himself. He said that he had just graduated from a hotel management school in Geneva and that the plan was for him to work for three years as a sommelier before returning home to help his father run their own winery and restaurant in Bordeaux. I asked him about the size of their winery production. It produced 33,000 cases of premium Bordeaux. I knew enough to know that producing 33,000 cases of premium Bordeaux was impressive.

I told him that I'd call him back. In the meantime, I called Annette and gave her the name of the winery and asked her if she could check out Bernard's claims about his background. Annette was happy to hear my voice and indicated that it was nothing, since they routinely contacted wineries to buy wine for their two hotels. Before we finished, she said, "Don't worry. This is easy, and I will say nothing to Jean Pierre." She, again, wanted to convey that she knew Jean Pierre and I had had a fling.

Within days, Annette called back and confirmed every detail Bernard had shared with me. Only then did I call Bernard back to let him know when I would be available. He chose a restaurant in Louisville, owned by someone he'd helped with his wine list. When I said that Louisville was three hours away, he said that if Julie Anne and I could take the bus early, he would drive us back to Berea. When I asked why Julie Anne needed to accompany me, he said, "You don't know me! It's best to have a chaperone."

I didn't even tell Julie Anne. I took the bus alone. When he met me at the bus station, I told him that I didn't need a chaperone and that I'd found out that my aunt and uncle in Paris were familiar with his father's winery.

I never said anything about being raised in a refugee camp nor did I explain that it was what had spurred Annette and Antoine to find my family in the first place. I kept those details to myself.

The evening was enjoyable, and Bernard behaved like a true gentleman. He was smart, sophisticated, and handsome. I was then nineteen and he was twenty-three. For the most part, I tended to think of men my age or a year older. The following week, he called me and proposed visiting me in Berea, where he would cook for the two of us, and we could share a bottle of his family winery's top wine. I informed him that I didn't have a place for him to cook nor a place to have dinner afterward.

He told me he'd pick me up and take me somewhere. I tried to tell him that he could park his car right in front of the dorm, but he said that wouldn't work. I wondered if he knew one of the girls and didn't want to accidentally run into her. When I saw him, he was driving a pickup truck loaded with all kinds of stuff. After I hopped into the truck, he drove me ten miles out of town into a wooded area. By the time he finished unloading, I figured out that he was planning to erect a tent, cook in it, and then set up a table for our dinner.

The picnic was first class in every respect. After we finished the wine-marinated quails with glazed maroon carrots, we devoured slices of French tarte Tatin, an upside-down apple tart. We lay down next to each other under a huge tree. Afterward, we had coffee that Bernard had brought in a thermos. Before we left, he poured me cognac in a crystal liqueur glass. It was smooth and delicious, but also too strong for me. Little by little, I'd forgotten about our age difference. He possessed a younger spirit, albeit with a very sophisticated touch.

It took two more dinners before we made out at his tastefully furnished apartment in Richmond. Between Jean Pierre, Julie Anne, and my biology classes, I had become a different person, with liberal ideas and ever-more discriminating taste. Definitely, I was no longer in Jordan. I was in different circumstances that allowed me to make different choices. I decided to follow the teachings of Imam Ali, the fourth successor to Prophet Mohammed. He allowed his soldiers to practice temporary marriages during war. I told myself, conveniently, that sex in Europe and America was equally OK.

I was very open with Bernard. I told him that I liked him a lot but that I was not the marrying type just then. He said the same. He was kinder: He said that he could change his mind if I happened to change mine. I told him that I didn't intend to risk an accidental pregnancy or take any pills, like one of my friends did. I added in plain English, "I am a rhythm girl." He said, "Your body is your own. I just share it briefly, as you do mine."

The relationship lasted three and a half years, during which I didn't date anyone else, American or otherwise. Two months before my graduation, he told me that duty called for him to go back to Bordeaux to assume his duties at the winery. He invited me to go back with him and "see your aunt." I said nothing, yet my silence said a lot—mostly a sense of inevitable loss. He said that he'd be back in six months to visit. I told him that by then I would have moved to Ann Arbor to study human physiology for my master's at the University of Michigan.

It then dawned on him that I was graduating in two months. He paused and said, "No, I'm not leaving. I want to see you graduate and attend your commencement." And so we continued to be monogamous for another two months. It was a most exhilarating yet serene relationship, defined by a deep care and even love for each other, but with a realization that neither of us was ready to settle down.

Before I saw him for the last time, I explained my relationship with the Allards. He told me that he had known every detail for some time, as his parents and the Allards had become friends as a result of Annette's call two years earlier. I said, "Somehow, I feel that the Allards are as much my parents as my biological parents are. They were supposed to attend my commencement, but unfortunately Antoine broke his ankle. I'm glad you have decided to stay."

Bernard prepared a special evening to celebrate my graduation. Without letting me know, he invited five of my girlfriends and their dates to a most gorgeous dinner. He had already set up two tents in the woods, one to cook in and another to dine in. I doubt that any of the guests had ever experienced such an elaborate and delicious dinner. We spent the night in the woods. It was an all-night affair, swarmed with intense emotions and lovemaking. We knew it was the end of a caring but realistic relationship that contained most of the perimeters of permanence, yet short of the proper time context.

Bernard and I wrote to each other, but we never suggested getting together again. Without saying it, we both realized that either it was going to be marriage or nothing. In the end, it was simply fond and loving memories.

Annette wrote to me with two pieces of good news: Bernard's parents spoke very highly of me, and Jean Pierre was seeing a pharmacist. I told her that there was no way I would miss Jean Pierre's wedding, if that was to happen. And teasingly, I added, "After all, we are brother and sister." Annette wrote back and said, "Yes, you are."

Chapter 7

At Michigan, my daydreaming transferred from Jean Pierre to Bernard. Jean Pierre's influence had been special, brief as it was. It was my initial sexual experience, a caring one, with pleasant memories. While what took place during the second summer in Paris was brief, its memories lingered in my mind for a long time, until Bernard replaced them with a present and a more mature exchange. My reaction to separating from Bernard was identical to my reaction when I returned to Amman after my first summer in Paris. I started dwelling on Bernard's lovemaking, just as I did on Jean Pierre's. I isolated myself to study and study hard.

I was eager to reach Ann Arbor. It was my second American city to visit, Louisville having been the first. I wondered what it would be like in comparison to Berea. It was not as green, nor as charming; although a small town, its small structures made the most salient impression. That didn't bother me, since I was looking forward to starting my master's program—a level I had never imagined I'd be able to attain.

I was friendly to my classmates but somewhat aloof. Two months into the first semester, I noticed a female student who was taking two of my four graduate courses. Her name was Rachel Shahak; her name in class was called right ahead of mine, Yara Shaheen. And we were both A students.

At the end of the semester, when I went to look up my grades for one of the courses, Rachel was there. She said, "Why are you here? You know you got an A." I said, "And why you are here? You know you got an A." She laughed. It was a very carefree and natural laugh, and I liked it.

Rachel looked at me smiling and said, "If you have time, I know a new place that serves great Turkish coffee."

"And why would I drink Turkish coffee?" I exclaimed, feeling that I was being stereotyped.

"Aren't you Lebanese or Palestinian? My uncle says you're probably Palestinian, since the name Yara is used in Palestine more often."

"I am Palestinian," I told her. "And you're Jewish American. You don't need to ask how I know. Rachel is surely a Jewish name; Shahak is either Jewish or Yiddish." She nodded in agreement and smiled. I smiled back, feeling that Rachel and I had made a connection.

Rachel took me in her fancy sports car, a brand-new Corvette. We both had Turkish coffee and wonderful hand-prepared baklava. The coffee was OK, but nowhere as good as my mother's. Rachel turned out to be charming and interesting. She was my first friend at Michigan, and nothing like Julie Anne. Rachel was an intellectual, very sharp and very organized. She was cute, and at 5'4," she was three inches shorter than me.

When we met for the third time, I told her about Bernard. She was surprised. She said that she didn't expect a Palestinian girl to be that liberated. She then told me that she didn't have a real boyfriend but that she was having sexual relations with two men, and that one of them was not Jewish. The Jewish man was back in her hometown, in Pittsburgh. The other one she had just met here at the University of Michigan: It was a teaching assistant, Jason, in one of our physiology classes. Rachel also volunteered that she was the one who had hit on him, rather than the other way around.

When she asked me if I was available to meet someone, I told her that I was not and that I preferred things happening on their own. She accused me of taking myself too seriously and suggested that I should adopt her attitude that sex was fun and that it deserved to be shared with "wholesome and attractive men." I told her to each her own and that neither of us needed to judge the other.

The following semester, Rachel and I had two courses together. We became best friends. When she asked me what I planned to do after my MS degree, I said that I intended to go for my PhD. "What for, to make $30,000 a year?" she asked. She told me that since her father was a physician, she'd decided to become a patent attorney, servicing medical and pharmaceutical companies. "I think I can make $100,000 a year," she added.

Although the sum she mentioned was considerable, it didn't impact my thinking. Slowly, Rachel's words started influencing me. I thought that with $100,000 I'd be able to build my parents an upscale three-bedroom house with two bathrooms.

When I talked to my father, I asked him if he could imagine living in a new and modern house. He said it would be the greatest thing that could happen to him since my birth and the birth of my brother. "I want a big house with high ceilings and a small library, to be able to read and write uninterrupted. I can imagine writing my poetry in an open and freer atmosphere," he said. After giving it deeper thought, I decided that if I could manage building a house for my family in Jordan, I wouldn't feel guilty for associating with the Allards. They were my parallel family, but by then I had a closer affinity with them than my real parents.

I told Rachel about my relationship with the Allards. I told her that I was very sorry that they hadn't been able to make it to my commencement at Berea. She invited me to accompany her to celebrate Purim on March 17. I told her I'd never known any Jewish families, nor did I know much about Jewish holidays. She said that her immediate family was very secular and that they mainly celebrated Jewish holidays to stay in touch with other members of the extended family.

Then she said, "I've already spoken to my father about you, and he is dying to meet you. I love my father; he is so neat. I think you'll like him, too." I told her that I looked forward to visiting her family but didn't want to stick out as a non-Jew in a Jewish celebration. But she convinced me, and I accepted.

On the day of Purim, we drove in Rachel's Corvette after we finished our classes. It took us three hours and forty-five minutes to reach Pittsburgh. When we arrived, Dr. Joseph Shahak and Rachel's mother, Sara, welcomed me with open arms. After we showered and went down to sit with them on their enclosed porch, the first thing Dr. Shahak said was, "Rachel told me that your parents live in a refugee camp after having lost your house in Jafa. I want you to know that I am deeply sorry; they deserve better. They deserve to be free and prosperous."

I didn't know what to say. I told him that, despite the fact all of us were raised in a refugee camp, we considered ourselves to be fortunate, as there were people in the camp and around the world who neither could afford food nor shelter. He looked at me and said, "You know what I mean. As a Jew and a humanitarian, I think you deserve better." I said, "Look at it this way; if it wasn't for the refugee camp, Rachel and I might never have met! Something to thank the camp for."

To this day, I can't tell if my visit changed anything. Dr. Shahak was particularly kind, and I had the impression that his opinion had been there all along. Above all, what I know is that I didn't notice that there was Purim. Everyone was drinking and so was I. I had a chance to meet Rachel's handsome brother, Michael. He was studying sociology at the University of Denver, both of which—his major and the choice of school—did not meet with the approval of his father. Yale hadn't accepted him to do his undergraduate work. Rachel had gone to Yale. When Michael asked me to visit him in Denver, Dr. Shahak told him that he didn't think I would accept. "She's Rachel's kind, not yours," he said.

I spent a wonderful four nights being wined, dined, and celebrated. Dr. Shahak told me that I was the second Palestinian he had ever met, and he was so pleased I could visit. He'd met the first Palestinian at Harvard, where he earned his medical degree. Later, he went back to Harvard to take four nuclear science courses, one of them under a Palestinian American professor who taught a decontamination course. After he retired from medicine, he built a nuclear decontamination facility near Pittsburgh. It was a lucrative enterprise and had secured large contracts from the defense department for seven years per contract.

He extended an invitation to my parents to visit. I told him that my father might, but since my mother would not, a visit would unfortunately be out of the question. My father had promised my mother not to travel alone after his ten-month stay in France. I told Dr. Shahak that my other parents, the Allards, were planning to attend my commencement at Michigan. I could tell he was aware of my relationship to the Allards. He also extended an invitation to them to visit him and Sara in Pittsburgh as well.

After my first visit, Rachel and I became even closer. She had no sisters and was not close to Michael. I made several trips with Rachel and, invariably, I was treated like a queen, but above all Dr. Shahak and I engaged in discussing varied subjects. I found him to be very learned and considerate. On a couple of occasions, I socialized with relatives of his who held extremist pro-Israel views, but he invariably took my side of the argument.

After Rachel and I finished our first year at Michigan, I visited the Shahaks in Pittsburgh for two weeks. It was during those weeks that Dr. Shahak broached the subject of studying law, specifically at Harvard. When I raised my concern that I couldn't afford Harvard, even if I were to get a full-tuition scholarship, he asked me not to worry and to see what was possible after I had applied and gotten an offer.

I was already thinking of the possibility of building my parents a roomier house; I didn't need much convincing to try. It was Rachel who told me later that there were three professors from Harvard who did research at her father's facility and that her father had endowed a chair at Harvard in the field of decontamination. Within two months of my visit, Rachel and I were both accepted at Harvard Law, provided we maintained a minimum A-minus average during our second and final year at Michigan. I learned later that Dr. Shahak had made sure that our applications received priority. Two weeks later, Rachel told me that her father got me a lucrative job translating technical Arabic into English, which sounded adequate to take care of my other expenses.

I pinched myself: first the Allards and now the Shahaks. On one visit to the Shahaks, we were joined by two attorneys for dinner: one older, Marvin, who was accompanied by his wife, and another much younger, David, who was alone. Dr. Shahak asked David if he was ready to settle down. I snickered because that was a routine conversation in Amman. People often asked how soon a man intended to marry.

David asked about my snicker. I didn't mind telling him what I was thinking. He said, "That figures. I guess we've been doing it from way back then."

"You mean the Jews?" I asked.

"Yes, the Jews. How did you decide I was Jewish?" I snickered again and said, "Your face looks European, but you have other Semitic features." He looked around the table and gazed at me. "And what could those features be?" he asked.

When I told him that I'd share those with Rachel, he said, "This isn't fair. Just as in law, which you will be studying soon, when one opens a subject then the other side has the right to probe into it." I looked at David and blushed. Rachel didn't come to my help; she also smilingly said that I was expected to explain myself. After hesitating, I said, "You must take into consideration that I am a human physiology student and observe features others don't.

"Before I say what the feature is, I want to explain myself openly, and possibly in an incriminating way. I believe that human beings have a tendency to discriminate against 'other kinds,' and only their upbringing, training, and intellect bring them up to being mostly indiscriminate and egalitarian. It took some self-sensitization to bring myself to an acceptable, though by no means sublime, level."

I continued after a brief pause, during which Dr. Shahak smiled and winked at me approvingly. "Now that I have expressed that neither I nor most people are fully sensitized, I will share that it is the well-endowed thighs that define Jews and Arabs alike."

Except for David, everyone at the table took my confession and characterization in stride, smiled, and looked at each other, with Dr. Shahak and Marvin inspecting their thighs. Marvin looked at me and said, "I guess you're right. I never checked my thighs out before. They look more robust than average." David looked at me and said, "I think you owe me a thorough discussion regarding your perception of Jewish men." It was clear that he intended to get to know me better.

A month later, I had dinner with David in Pittsburgh. It was a very fancy steak house. When I told David that I thought half of the clientele were Jewish, he said that I was too forward in looking at thighs. David was a graduate of the University of Pennsylvania law school. His undergraduate degree was in industrial engineering, and his law practice dealt with metallurgy and industrial alloys.

We went out five times, and on the sixth date we made love. It was passionate and venturesome. I had never considered making love to a Jew before then. It is not that I hated Jews; I just hadn't known any. My relationship with David, on top of my relations with the Shahaks, helped me humanize an ethnic group I had looked on as an enemy. I guess I still had Middle Eastern values; marital sex was the ultimate test for pleasure and premarital sex was the ultimate sin.

David was always complimenting me on my looks and the way I dressed. I didn't tell him anything about Annette continuously sending me Parisian clothing. The relationship with David lasted until I graduated from Michigan. He never offered to accompany Joseph and Sara Shahak to my commencement, not even when I told him that the Allards were coming all the way from Paris.

I was told why later: The Jewish *shadkhan* (Jewish marriage broker) had found him a prospective bride. In retrospect, he was considerate, having realized that our relationship was ending. The last two times we got together he refrained from having sex with me.

The Allards and the Shahaks met at the commencement and bonded right away. Annette whispered in my ear, "They are very nice Jews." I told her in the future to say they are nice without referring to their ethnicity. "I don't see anything wrong with that. You can call me a nice French woman anytime." I told her there was a nuanced difference: The Jews were historically isolated from their Christian neighbors. Then Annette asked why I didn't say that they were isolated from their Muslim neighbors. I said, "Believe it or not, they are not" and that the Muslim conflict with Israel was political in nature. Annette promised to investigate my claims.

Everything went right at the commencement. I now had a master's degree from Michigan and was proceeding to Harvard. As with Bernard, my relationship with David had come to an easy end, since neither of us intended to marry the other. Above all, I felt that I had three families now—two of them rich and influential. Occasionally, I used to remind myself not to be carried away when it came to the Shahaks, and to wait for further proof.

PART III

1970

Chapter 8

The summer was relaxing. I had the choice to be anywhere in the United States. Our admission into Harvard Law was secured, since Rachel and I had both maintained an A average at Michigan and scored in the top 5 percent on the LSAT. I politely turned down Rachel's invitation to spend the summer with her at her parents' home. Dr. Shahak called me to tell me that the invitation was his as well as Sara's. Yet I decided not to overdo it. I recalled an Arabic saying: "If your friend is made of honey, don't lick it all at one time."

I called Rachel and told her that I was interested in sleeping with different types of men. I was intent on liberating myself from my own inhibitions. Rachel told me that life wasn't a sampling experiment. I told her that I knew I wasn't a racist but that I needed to elevate myself, not only to look at everyone similarly but to treat them similarly. I added that I was thinking of going to Dearborn, home to the largest Arab American community in Michigan and the United States, to observe how Arab Americans intermingled with other races.

When Rachel asked me how I was going to find out, I told her that I was going to visit as many Arab American supermarkets as possible and just watch the shoppers. Rachel liked the idea and asked if she could accompany me. I wasn't expecting her company, but I welcomed it on the spot.

When we got to Dearborn, I had with me the names of three supermarkets. As soon as we arrived at the first one, I could see one Black couple and a solo Black man. Rachel and I got close to the couple, but right away I told Rachel to pass them. I told her that they didn't qualify. "Why not, they're Black?" she asked. I told her that they were Sudanese Arabs, which I could tell from their dialect. Rachel didn't understand. I had to explain to her that I didn't look at the Sudanese as being Black; I considered them to be Arab and that only American Blacks were Black to me. My own statement raised a question in my mind: why the difference? My conclusion was that I thought of Arab Blacks in an Arab context and of American Blacks in an American context.

Rachel looked bewildered at my rationale. I realized that it was much more than a color thing; it was a combination of factors, including ethnicity and familiarity. I told Rachel that familiarity was a bigger factor than ethnicity and that my sampling was designed to familiarize myself with Black Americans and Asians.

After analyzing my own subconscious stratification of my attractions, I became the questioner when I found out that Rachel hadn't slept with people of different racial and ethnic backgrounds either. At that point, I tried to prod Rachel to get ahead of me in the sampling effort.

That summer was delightful. I managed to visit Rachel three times and would go there on short notice, especially when the weather got hot in Ann Arbor. My small apartment was not air-conditioned, and the Shahak house was.

When it was time to move to Cambridge, where Harvard was, Rachel and I didn't have to work hard to set things up. Dr. Shahak's assistant took care of the logistics associated with our move. She leased a three-bedroom house for Rachel and me to share. Dr. Shahak was generous; he paid 50 percent of the rent, ostensibly to cover the cost of his using the third bedroom whenever he visited his firm's scientific collaborators at Harvard. Rachel told me that her father didn't intend to use the third bedroom at all; he just didn't want me to feel that his 50 percent contribution was charity. By college students' standards, we were well-housed.

I proposed to Rachel that we lease out the third bedroom. When she said she preferred to not have another roommate, I revealed to her that I was hoping a female student with a different racial and ethnic background would live with us. Jokingly, Rachel asked if I was interested in women, and I answered very dismissively that I was not. I explained that I wanted to learn more about other cultures, and hopefully another roommate would allow for that.

Rachel was understanding and supportive. She told me then that she was socializing with the families of two of her father's Black coworkers, and she had a lot in common with them. "It all depends on socioeconomic status," she said. It became clear to me why: They were Dr. Shahak's peers, both PhD holders, graduates of Harvard and Cornell. I was beginning to realize that in America, socioeconomic status was also a factor in how people were perceived.

We proceeded with my proposal and, based on the location and quality of the house, we had a lot of interested responses. We waited until we got what looked like a compatible prospect. She was a third-year engineering student, very good looking, with a pleasant attitude. Her mother was a high school teacher, and her father was a school district superintendent. Her name was Jameela—an Arab name—and her brother was Jamal. Jamal was finishing his doctorate in psychology at New York University.

The choice of roommate was too good to be true, yet it involved an ulterior motive. As we got to know Jameela better, Rachel and I decided that it was ethically incumbent upon us to share with her the reason behind our interest. At first, Jameela reacted strongly and told us that she wanted to move out. I apologized to Jameela and assumed all the blame, trying to exonerate Rachel as being a reluctant participant.

Fortunately for us, Jameela couldn't find another acceptable accommodation and decided to stay through the whole semester. Again, Dr. Shahak came to our rescue after he heard what we had done; he came over and invited all three of us to dinner. Jameela initially turned the invitation down, but Dr. Shahak insisted and got his way.

Dr. Shahak didn't hold back. He started by describing how he was tutored in decontamination by a Palestinian American professor. He then found his way of relating the Palestinian struggle to the African American struggle. That gave him a reason to mention the many Black professionals he was collaborating with. Jameela was no dummy; she knew well why Dr. Shahak was bringing up such pointers. Nevertheless, she enjoyed the evening and looked more relaxed afterward.

Within a few days, Jameela insisted on inviting me and Rachel to a reciprocal dinner. We tried to resist by insisting on going Dutch. She wouldn't accept. She took us to an upscale Arabic restaurant, another sign of reconciliation. During dinner, she came straight out and said that she had changed her mind and that she wanted to continue to be our roommate. "Provided it is OK with you," she said. That was music to our ears. Jokingly, I told her that I would accept if she would take us out to this restaurant once a month.

After that, life proceeded much more harmoniously. There was the occasional snappy behavior between roommates, but it rarely afflicted more than one of us at the same time. Rachel would say, "Give her space; it's her turn." I'm sure she said the same to Jameela when I acted erratically.

Rachel put in seven hours of study every evening, and I averaged eight. I attributed the difference to the fact that Rachel was still more versed in the English language than I was. Jameela applied herself no more than four and a half hours each night. She had transferred to Harvard from Rutgers, after receiving a BS in physics and math, where she had maintained an A average.

We followed a routine schedule. One early morning, as I was jogging, I ran into Moens Thomasson—the same know-it-all Moens Thomasson from Berea College. I saw him looking at me. I stopped, after recognizing his slimmer build. He looked at me, and I looked at him without either of us saying anything at first. "You are Yara of Palestine!" he said. "And you are Moens of Kentucky," I answered. "You look different," I added.

He volunteered that he had just come back from a two-month stay in Europe. When I asked if he had visited Iceland, the homeland of his Scandinavian father, he didn't answer. After he reminded me that he was in his third year of law school, I took the opportunity to ask him if he cared to have a cup of coffee. He immediately said yes. Somehow his slimmed-down physique made him appear softer and more approachable. Moens might have changed, I thought, and this presented another opportunity for me.

After I finished my jog, I went back home to talk to Rachel. I found her fixing omelets for the three of us, with onions, mushrooms, and ripened tomatoes. I showed her how to add pomegranate molasses to give it a slight tang. She didn't want to be interrupted, but I insisted. "I think I've found my candidate," I said. When she asked what kind of candidate, I told her how I ran into Moens and that he looked and sounded much different from when I knew him at Berea. "He really looks handsome," I added.

Rachel finished the omelet and asked me to serve myself and sit at the dining table. When I asked about Jameela, Rachel said that she wanted to talk to me alone first. "Yara, you're starting to sound like a white plantation owner in the Old South. You shouldn't look at Moens as a piece of ass. Whether he is gentle and considerate or not, he is not a commodity. You ought to have feelings for him before you engage in sex." Rachel's statement surprised me. I went silent for a while, having my preliminary plans so casually deflated. I looked at her intently and said, "You're 100 percent right. I honestly didn't have plans to have sex with him, to start with. I do want to try dating him and see how things develop. Did you even think that I'd sleep with him if I didn't develop feelings for him? Never."

Rachel hollered at Jameela to join us. Jameela tasted the omelet and said that she liked its tangy taste. The subject of Moens got shifted to small talk about food. I told Rachel that I planned to fix "upside-down," the Palestinian national dish, for her and her parents, if her mother didn't mind me using her kitchen. I added, "Listen, Rachel, you said that you wanted Jameela to visit you in Pennsylvania next time we go, so why don't I make it when Jameela comes with us to Pittsburgh?"

I then took the initiative to call Moens to have coffee together.

We had coffee four times—mostly arranged by me—before Moens invited me to a performance by the Harvard symphony. I accompanied him to three symphony performances but never developed a feeling for it. When I told Moens how I felt, he insisted that if I was to continue listening to classical music I'd nurture an appreciation for it.

Just like I promised Rachel, I checked on my feelings toward him to find them getting stronger, regardless of my feelings for classical music. I liked his carefree attitude, sharing with me detailed information about his background. The next time he invited me to a performance, he also invited me to his apartment. He said that his roommate would be out of town that evening and that he planned to fix me his mother's favorite dish. Again, the performance was acceptable but didn't arouse any new admiration for classical music. I still preferred Middle Eastern music.

Nevertheless, we were gradually getting to know each other better. I told him about my family, and he told me about his aspirations. He already had an offer from the NAACP. He also told me that his desire was to become a Supreme Court justice and that his becoming deputy council with the NAACP was meant to be a stepping stone; he said that he didn't believe in the methods of the NAACP, and that Blacks needed to be left alone to either make it or fail in life. I wasn't sure how I felt about Moens's disregard for programs that helped the Black American community make up for what they suffered under slavery and beyond.

When we got to Moens's apartment, it looked more modern than our home but much smaller. I sat down in the living room diagonally across from him, with my tight skirt all the way up my legs. Moens spoke first. "I've never been out with someone like you before." When I asked what he meant by that, he said, "I've never made love to a brown woman, ever. Actually, I don't make love to Black girls at all. I only sleep with white girls. You see, my father is an Icelandic white." I looked at him, noticing that much of his softness and gentle approach had almost totally evaporated. While soft spoken, now he sounded self-righteous and self-centered.

I looked at him with amazement and some disgust, yet said nothing. He looked at me and said, "I don't want to be rude. Both you and I know why we're here. I like you. You're very good looking, and I am making an exception because of your looks. I don't mind making an exception in your case." My flabbergasted reaction was clearly visible on my face. He didn't give me a chance to react before he said that he needed to go into the bedroom.

Within two minutes he called me to follow him. He was sitting at the edge of the bed, naked, with his legs wide open. I looked at him, resigned to not accommodate him. While I was disgusted at his weird attitude, I became slightly confused and adopted an inquisitive but detached attitude toward what I considered to be a confused man. When he saw me looking at his crotch, he said, "Do you like what you see? You can start by giving me a blow job."

I walked toward him ever so slowly, gazing at his crotch, dragging my feet, and stopping almost between his legs. I said in a very slow and hushed tone, "You must have forgotten that I have a master's in human physiology. Yes, you are endowed but not by any satisfactory standards." I was trying to insult him and exaggerating at the same time to make my point.

I looked him in the eyes intently, in a condescending way, to pause before I summoned my courage to slap him hard on the face. Then I said, "You are a mess of a man, if you even deserve to be referred to as a man. You are a mixed-up man who deserves to be branded as prejudiced and a misogynist."

Moens was shocked at my reaction, especially at my slapping him. He looked at me, speechless. "Get dressed and go fuck yourself," I added, hurrying to leave his apartment. I was almost hyperventilating as I walked crisply away. All of a sudden, I got ahold of my emotions and stopped three blocks from his apartment. I sat on the edge of a large flowerpot. Moens's behavior made no sense as all. When we'd talked before, he had strangely and unexpectedly shared so much with me.

Little by little, he'd told me that Berea would not have admitted him if they knew how much money he was receiving from his father. He added that he was following a well-devised plan: first Berea, then Harvard, then the NAACP, and finally the Supreme Court. The first two came through perfectly. Now he was working on the third and fourth. In hindsight, what amazed me was how cavalier he acted in sharing all of this with me and then for him to risk it all by behaving the way he had.

I could barely finish collecting my thoughts when I recalled another statement of his, now alarming, that earlier I'd taken as a joke. He said that he felt he was a white person and wished he was physically white. All of this made me think that I could not have been the first woman he slighted. He must have done similar things to other people, regardless of gender.

When I got home, Rachel and Jameela were studying. Rachel came out into the living room, eager to find out about my date. She quickly saw my ashen and angry face. As I sat in the chair and lowered my head all the way down between my legs, Rachel became concerned and asked what was wrong. I didn't answer her at first, but she kept repeating the same question, raising her voice, which alerted Jameela.

Jameela, having overheard Rachel's inquiry, also asked what was wrong. I took a deep breath, asked them to sit down, and said, "I am going to tell you everything." I proceeded to describe in full detail what had happened that evening. Despite my detailed descriptions, Jameela interpreted Moens as a white racist who didn't want to sleep with brown women. Apparently, she could only think of racists as being white.

Finally, I said, "He is a weird, self-hating Black."

Jameela stood up and said, "You mean you had a date with a Black man, but what makes you refer to him as a self-hating Black? Are you not jumping to a premature conclusion?"

"Yes, and is there anything wrong with a quick conclusion?" I snapped at her. She said, "Well, I don't go out that often with Black men. I prefer Hispanics." I gave her a surprised look.

She then explained that it wasn't that she was not attracted to Black men, but that it was easier for her to tell if Hispanic Don Juans were sincere and on the level. I just nodded my head, trying to conceal my dislike for her characterization. After this, I went to bed totally disappointed with the whole evening and with myself. Within a few weeks of the encounter with Moens, I felt I had to tell Jameela the full details of my feelings, my motives, and my encounter. This time around, she was more understanding and even teasingly promised that she and I could plan to double-date two Black men.

Chapter 9

I didn't realize that I would get mad at Moens: I did get mad, with nothing but pure indignation. Within a few days I marginalized his actions and got mad at myself. It was a different feeling. I could not recall harboring a similar feeling in the past. Prudently, I told Rachel and Jameela that I was in a sour mood and for them to stay out of my way. Both tried to soothe my self-blaming attitude but failed. Fortunately, my studies didn't suffer.

Within four days of the incident, I was shocked to run into Moens waiting outside our house. I kept walking and he walked after me. "I could have called you but didn't want to risk you hanging up on me," he said. "I genuinely want to apologize. I was crude and totally insensitive." I stopped, turned around, and looked him straight in the eyes and said, "OK, you apologized. I don't ever want to see you again. You need to avoid me or else you'll be sorry." He looked at me and said nothing, but I could see concern all over his face. His worried look didn't alleviate my sense of failure and sense of blame. I left without him following me.

I shared the news of my encounter with Rachel and Jameela. Rachel immediately suggested that if worse came to worse we could consult with her father and that he could ask the Harvard administration to intervene, if necessary. Jameela pointed out that Moens had done nothing yet. Jameela instead suggested that she confront Moens, explaining that he might relate better to someone who had shared his experience of racism.

I felt better, and we all decided not to do anything for the time being. A week later, Moens confronted me again, this time pleading with me just to listen to him and that if I didn't like what I heard he'd never bother me again. At first, I kept walking without responding. "I'm not trying to have a relationship with you; I'm only trying to make sure that neither of us will hurt the other in the future," Moens said.

I couldn't tell what he meant. I felt that revealing the episode between us could hurt him, but I didn't know how he could hurt me. He aroused both my curiosity and my suspicions. When I asked him dismissively to explain what was on his mind, he said that he couldn't tell me anything in the open. He suggested we have pizza together, but I declined. We finally agreed to meet before class, at 7:30 the following morning, on campus.

When we got together, Moens was appreciative, and he expressed it openly. He started by telling me that he needed to share things with me he only shared with his mother, in order to impress upon me how important it was for neither of us to bad-mouth the other. When I said that there was nothing he could bad-mouth me about, he said, "You know, when rumors start spreading, you can't know how they impact your career." I looked at him again dismissively. He then added that he was referring to himself.

He proceeded to tell me that his dream was to become the second Black Supreme Court justice, after Thurgood Marshall, and that he felt that he got one major step closer last month by the NAACP offer to be their deputy legal counsel. He repeated that he had been offered a high-level job with the NAACP upon his graduation from Harvard Law. When I asked why the NAACP would offer someone like him a high-level legal position, he said, "What do you mean? I'm Black and will have a law degree from Harvard."

I stood up in disgust and said, "What kind of nonsense is this?" He paused as he looked at me with disappointment and said, "This is why I wanted to get together with you: to ask you not to say any untrue and scurrilous things about me. I am going to be the deputy NAACP legal counsel."

I was convinced he was faking it. I got up from my chair, and when he tried unsuccessfully to get me to sit down again, I looked at him and said, "You're altogether fake, and you're trying to play with my mind. It's not going to work." I started walking away when he said, "You Palestinian bitch."

At that point, I couldn't tell whether I'd done the right thing by meeting with him or not. I was pleased that I'd confronted him, and his last insult convinced me that he'd sink to levels I couldn't stoop to. I needed to consult with Rachel again. When I told her what had happened, she told me that the whole thing didn't sound civilized, but not to worry about it. She suggested we consult Jameela. Jameela was much more concerned. She told us that, because he'd stooped to such a low level, she could think of a dozen things he could say and do, as he seemed not to be constrained by any ethical bounds. Again, we decided not to worry about it for the time being.

I heard nothing further from Moens. Five weeks after our encounter, Jameela left me a note that someone by the name of Wang Junxi had called. I waited until she came home and asked if

Junxi had said anything about why he was contacting me. Jameela said that she thought he was a law school classmate.

When I called him back, he was coy. He answered that he had never met me and that he was an engineering student from Wuhan, China. When I asked him why he was calling me, he responded, "You know why I'm calling you." I told him that I'd never heard his name and that I didn't have anything to do with engineering. He then said that he had no time to play games. "It's either a yes or a no. I understand you like Chinese men." I said, "I like some men, and I don't care for others. What is this all about?" He then said that someone told him that I liked Chinese and Black men. At that point I was infuriated. "Stop this nonsense. I don't know what you're talking about," I said as I tried to hang up on him. He immediately said, "Don't worry. I'm ten times as rich as Moens! You know what I mean."

I slammed the phone down. I couldn't think straight as I thought about what Moens meant when he referred to rumors spreading. I got angry and agitated at first but slowly grew more concerned. I started shedding tears of sadness for the first time since I had left Amman. Jameela could hear me and rushed out of her bedroom to see what was going on. I couldn't bring myself to tell her what had happened between Junxi and me. I went into my room and lay on the bed, continuing to cry.

When Rachel got back, she also tried to find out what had happened, but to no avail. Two hours later I took a shower and then after, with wet hair, slowly repeated the phone conversation to them, almost verbatim. Both Rachel and Jameela were disturbed by what I told them. Jameela was the one who said that she expected Moens to react, but not to go that low. She then said, "I'll be damned if

I'm going let him get away with it." Rachel didn't know what to say. She kept silent for a long while before she said, "This is serious and requires careful consideration. Please don't do anything rash. Whatever we come up with, it must be 99 percent sure and decisive. We can't miss."

All three of us kept silent for a while. Jameela was the first to say, "Listen guys, in some cases the best defense is a good offense. Let's think of something we can pin on him. Yara, you know him from Berea; you must know something about him." Jameela's probe made me start thinking. "No, I don't know much about him, but I know several students who knew him well from the work program there," I answered.

Jameela asked me to take my time and make a list, and in the meantime to think of how they could be approached. Rachel said, "This is very serious. I think we should try and meet with them in person." When I wondered how, since they would have all left Berea, Rachel said that we could call the college and ask for their contact information from the alumni office.

In no time, I managed to get the contact information of all five students, and what was even more helpful was the fact that three of them were in New York City: one at Columbia, another at NYU, and a third at the New School. I called all three and managed to set up appointments with them for the following weekend. Rachel was the logistic and financial savior. She volunteered to pay for a group dinner after we had met each separately. She also volunteered the use of her car for the trip.

We were planning to start discrediting Moens by telling them how he was pretending to be the next NAACP deputy counsel. Then, to our surprise, Dr. Shahak called to report that he had checked with two sources and confirmed that what Moens said about soon becoming the deputy legal counsel was the truth.

I realized that confronting Moens was even more important than him smearing my reputation. Somehow, he had managed to get into Berea even though he didn't qualify as having been financially challenged; now he was assuming a high position with the NAACP. If someone so unethical could finagle himself into a job with the NAACP, why should the Supreme Court be beyond his reach? I asked myself.

Our New York meetings with Joanne and Summer, two of Moens's peers at Berea, were helpful but provided limited information. It wasn't until we met Laticia at the New School that we got a lead. Laticia told us that she'd had a four-month relationship with Moens and decided to break it off, so Moens spread a rumor that she stole one of his paintings. When Laticia confronted him, he kept insisting that she stole it. She lived through an agonizing situation for two months before a friend of hers happened to buy the same painting for $400 at a flea market. After further investigations and a description of Moens by the seller, Laticia confronted him again. Buttressing her arguments with the records of the purchase, she forced Moens to call several students and place an ad in the student paper that he'd found his missing painting and that it had never been stolen in the first place.

In the evening at the group dinner, the other two shared similar horrifying experiences with Moens. Rachel, Jameela, and I needed to figure out what to do with the information we had gathered. We couldn't come out with anything certain. Once again, we had to consult with an experienced hand, namely Dr. Shahak.

Although not an attorney, Dr. Shahak expressed his opinion

that I had to prove that Moens was the source of the rumor about me. Then and only then could we use the testimony of the three others as supporting evidence. It was certainly a disappointment: We'd hoped to get what we needed.

It was time to regroup. We thought about Junxi's call and were about to dismiss it when I got another call, this time from a delivery driver. When he called, he asked me to choose the time and he'd choose the place. When I asked what he knew about me, he told me that "the other guy showed me your picture." I slammed the phone down twice when I hung up.

Rachel and Jameela could see my disturbed reaction. For three days afterward, I barely talked to my roommates, even refusing to go over my study material with Rachel. I could tell that Rachel was worried that my attitude would impact my studies.

This time Jameela came to the rescue. She told Rachel and me that she had to confront Moens. We asked her not to act irrationally. "Don't worry about me," Jameela replied. "He's a Black man from Kentucky, and I'm a Black woman from New Jersey."

Chapter 10

Even though Rachel and I tried to convince her not to, Jameela decided to confront Moens. She didn't even bother to call him. She went to his apartment. She knocked on the door, and Moens opened it. She was well-dressed, with every intention of using her arguments, good looks, and personality to dominate the conversation. Moens had no way of recognizing her. When he asked if he could help her, she introduced herself as my roommate.

Moens looked Jameela up and down and said, "Are you together?" The way Jameela told it to us later, it sounded like he was suggesting we had a lesbian relationship. Jameela snapped, "No, I'm her roommate. And I'm here to discuss the rumors you're spreading about Yara. If you don't stop this, you'll be sorry."

"Sorry how?" Moens asked. "I don't have anything to do with it."

"Yes, you do, and you've done it before. Do you remember Laticia?" Moens looked at Jameela with bulging eyes and said, "You talked to Laticia!"

"Yes, we all told her what happened between you and Yara. We also told other acquaintances of yours. I'm not here to expose you. We're not interested in your past. I'm here to warn you not to press your luck and that you need to deny everything you've said about Yara and agree to never contact her in the future, or have anyone else contact her."

Moens invited Jameela in, insinuating that he wanted to discuss the matter in a civilized manner. Jameela was wearing a white wrap skirt. As she sat down, it opened and exposed her legs. "I like your legs. They look good," Moens said. Jameela immediately fixed her skirt and said, "They're not for your kind. And I'm only here to talk about your malicious rumors, nothing else."

Jameela could see that Moens was getting seriously agitated. While that was part of her intention, his facial expression started to look frightening. All of a sudden, he said, "You think you're better than me, you bitch." Jameela was nervous now, so she stood up casually and started walking slowly toward the door, and then sprinted. Moens jumped out of his chair, dove toward her, and managed to grab her by one ankle.

She fell on her back and instantly he was on top of her, with the flap of her skirt open to her crotch. Moens stripped her panties off with his two hands and in seconds he was raping her, with one of his palms covering her mouth. Jameela could barely scream before he reached a quick climax and the whole thing was over. Not only was she in shock; he, too, looked stupefied at what he had just done. He hurried into his bedroom, grabbed a large towel, and covered Jameela's exposed crotch.

Jameela was lying there motionless. It took her a couple of minutes to wipe herself partially clean, slip her panties on, and get up slowly, totally speechless, and then resume heading toward the front door. When she got home, she hurried to go to the bathroom, but both Rachel and I noticed her reddish and scraped cheek. We both stood up simultaneously to ask about it, but she locked the bathroom door.

We waited for over fifteen minutes. Rachel tried to listen through the shut door of the bathroom. She looked at me and whispered, "She's crying." I joined Rachel at the door to confirm this. We slowly went back into the living room, whispering to each other.

Forty-five minutes later, Jameela was still in the bathroom. Finally, I knocked hard on the door and said, "Jameela, what's going on? Rachel and I are worried sick. Why don't you come out and let us know you are all right before we break down the door."

Jameela answered and said that she would be out after taking a shower. Ten minutes later, she came out and sat down in the living room and started crying, looking down at the floor. She went through several labored sighs and said in a low voice, "He raped me." Rachel spoke, "Oh my god, you mean Moens?" said Rachel. "Yes, Moens. Who else?" said Jameela.

At that moment I felt like I had dropped into a bottomless hole. I realized that we'd started with one serious problem and ended up with a much more serious one. I didn't know what to do, and I felt terribly guilty for instigating everything by attempting to prove to myself that I didn't have any hidden prejudices. I had done this once before. I got a bottle of Chablis from the fridge and poured myself a full glass of wine. I couldn't recall that I'd ever consumed alcohol except with food. I offered the bottle to Rachel and Jameela. Jameela said it was a great idea. Rachel didn't want any.

Jameela got out of her chair and came toward me. She hugged me and said, "My period ended eight days ago; I'm safe. And don't blame yourself. I shouldn't have gone over there."

Rachel nodded her head approvingly, looked at me, and said, "What Jameela said is gracious and very important. If we start blaming each other, we won't be able to stay roommates or friends. We have to stick together and support each other."

Rachel and I agreed to wait for Jameela to say what she wanted to do. But for the next ten days, she didn't confide in either of us.

When Rachel and I came home after the last Friday law class, we found Jameela sobbing in the living room. I ran toward her, fearing the worst or some new problem. Jameela was now feeling angry at everything and everyone, including herself. She kept crying profusely as she tried to explain. Both Rachel and I were worried. I said, "Tell us what it is—did something new happen? You're scaring the hell out of us."

Jameela looked at me and said, "I love you both, but this isn't working. I haven't slept much since the incident. I have to get out of here. I want to drop out and go home, and hopefully I can come back next semester. Yara, you may have been right, He could easily be a self-hating Black. I have a feeling he wouldn't do to a white girl what he did to me. You sense it in his posture and his attitude."

Then Rachel told Jameela that it was natural for a traumatic experience to cause an emotional whiplash. "But it will get better," she said. "You won't forget, but it will get better."

Jameela insisted that staying at Harvard in the short term wouldn't be a good idea and would keep reminding her of the incident. Rachel disagreed and said that if Jameela went home she'd harbor the same feelings. But Jameela continued to insist that she needed to leave.

Rachel said, "You mean you intend to do nothing about the incident and have him get away with it?" I looked at both of them and said, "I think it is I who needs to leave. I'll move to Dearborn and work at one of the Arab American supermarkets. Who knows, maybe I'll even fulfill my mother's hopes of finding a Muslim Sunni husband."

Rachel gave me a most condescending look and then looked at Jameela and said, "Fine. You can both leave. And you know what? You both make me sick to my stomach. You have no guts and no survival instinct. Imagine if Jewish and Black people all along and the Palestinian people now had the same attitude: They'd all be extinct. Do whatever you want, and you don't have to let me know. I'm done." She picked up her purse and left in a hurry.

Jameela and I looked at each other in surprise at Rachel's words. Then both of us retreated to our bedrooms. Half an hour later, Jameela knocked on my door, carrying a small suitcase in her hand. I looked at the suitcase and said, "You're leaving?" When she said that she was, I asked if it was for good. She said that she didn't know but that she needed to clear her head back home in New Jersey.

Rachel came back five hours later. I could tell she was inebriated. She asked about Jameela. I told her exactly what Jameela had said: that she'd gone to New Jersey to clear her head. Rachel looked at me with her piercing eyes and said, "I don't think it's going to happen. New Jersey is polluted for the most part anyway. How about you? Are you going back to Palestine?"

I could tell then that she was more than just a little drunk. I took her by her arm and led her to her room and lay her down gently. I woke up four hours later to the sound of her throwing up. She could barely raise her head from the toilet. Ten minutes later, her glazed eyes looked clearer. She washed her face and wiped it dry and then combed her hair. She suddenly looked fully alert. She walked toward me, hugged me, and said, "I've heard of many Jews falling in love with Blacks, but falling in love with Palestinians—no, and you know why, because neither you nor her are pussies. I'm so sorry."

I hugged Rachel very tightly and started crying. "I've been so lucky so far," I said. "The Allards and you and your family have been the best things that have happened to me. I've been given more than I could possibly repay. I have an idea."

"What?" Rachel asked.

"How about if we go back to bed and head off to New Jersey in the morning?"

Rachel shook her head. "No, we're already awake. How about if we head off to New Jersey right away." We were in New Jersey at 6:45 in the morning, parking in front of Jameela's parents' house. Rachel said that although they might not be awake, they'd understand that we had come all the way from Cambridge through the night.

When we knocked on the door, it took a good three minutes for someone to open up. It was none other than Jameela's brother, Jamal. He didn't have to ask. He said, "You're Yara and Rachel." We didn't know what Jameela had told him, if anything, but he didn't seem too surprised to see us.

As I tried to shake Jamal's hand, he pulled it back and said, "Sorry, I just did my ablution." When he saw our surprise, he snickered and said, "I'm kidding. I did convert, but I'm Hanafi," referring to the most liberal sect of Sunni Islam.

After he led us to Jameela's bedroom, Rachel and I went in quietly. Jameela was sound asleep, in a twisted position, with her bed cover on the floor. I picked it up and covered her. I sat on one side of the bed and Rachel on the other. I gently said, "Jameela, you are under arrest for leaving without permission."

Jameela woke up and looked at us. After shaking her sleep off, she hugged us. She apologized and said that she didn't know what to do, and that she was glad we'd come to see her. She then said that if we stayed the night, she'd go back with us the following day. We were all relieved.

That day we visited with her family, including her handsome brother, Jamal. He told us that he was defending his dissertation in three months and expecting to graduate in six.

Early Sunday morning, we left for Cambridge. On the way, I proposed that we not talk about the issue with Moens for at least a week so that we could all catch up on our studies and try to normalize things. Both agreed. It was a practical suggestion, as Rachel and I helped each other catch up. Jameela was much more equipped. For the first time, she mentioned that she had already graduated with a degree in math and a minor in physics, which gave her some advantage over her engineering classmates.

I was the one again who proposed that we go out for dinner and decide whether we intended to take any action or skip it all together. No one else had called me since the delivery man, and I wondered if Moens was scared after he had raped Jameela. He had to be thinking that there were two potential witnesses who could level accusations against him.

But we didn't know what to do. We felt lost. It was not a sanguine feeling. Throughout our dinner, we paused a lot and spoke very little. In the end, it was Rachel who said, "I hate to propose this, but if you two have no objections, maybe, just maybe, we could consult my father." I'm sure she didn't expect me or Jameela to disagree. Neither of us did. We both found it a relief. Dr. Shahak was like a contract consultant. We welcomed the suggestion and asked

Rachel to arrange a dinner with her father, despite the fact we knew well that the good doctor would insist on paying.

The following week, we were taken to a very fancy restaurant. Dr. Shahak tried some levity. "I'm going to order a double Glenlivit, knowing the seriousness of the subject. Anyone care to join me?" We all opted for wine, which he chose: one superior to our usual and less expensive choices. Rachel opened the conversation by saying that she had summarized the situation altogether, but now she intended to tell it in detail, and that if Jameela objected to let her know. Jameela did not.

It was time for another double Glenlivit when Dr. Shahak said, "This is serious. I am sure, with Yara and Jameela and the three women in New York, there's no way you could lose the fight. The problem is the university. Politics impacts everyone, including Harvard. They are usually good, but not perfect. If they surmise that there could be irreparable damage, they'll sacrifice your interests in a New York minute. On the other hand, I can play two roles. The first entails my influence with Harvard and the second entails my influence with my banker. In other words, I will finance the whole thing if you are tough enough to withstand the pressure and remotely risk your education and the potential of not receiving your degrees from this institution."

All three of us looked at each other, smiling. I said that I would go with it; Jameela seconded my sentiment. Rachel said that she would help. I suggested that we leave it at that and savor our dinner before we reopen the subject the following week. "I like that, Yara; you know how to be patient," said Dr. Shahak.

"They call this prudently patient, and it is expressed in one word in Arabic. I'm sure there is parallel word in Hebrew," I said.

"What is the word in Arabic?" asked Dr. Shahak.

"For a man, it is *haleem*, and for a woman, it is *haleema*. You know Arabic is completely gender sensitive, like Hebrew," I added.

In all, it was a most productive dinner, with Dr. Shahak encouraging us to think carefully and plan for the short and long term. He promised his full support. Before he left, he asked that we proceed cautiously and to check with him if need be. "Rachel and Yara, you are both going to be attorneys—do not undertake anything that is even slightly illegal or even questionable," he said. I was sure he meant to include Jameela in his admonition as well.

Chapter 11

I don't recall all three of us being this happy and acting giddy at the same time. We decided to savor the feeling. Jameela said that she'd decided not to pursue Moens administratively or legally. Her argument was simple: It was going to be her word against his, and the popular sentiment at the time implied that only loose women got raped. She reminded us that she was graduating in less than a year, and after that she would devote all her time to going after Moens. I thought one of us would respond to Jameela with a different point of view. Instead, we all seemed to feel better that she was not pursuing Moens for the time being. Everyone, above all Rachel and me, seemed to momentarily relax, forgetting about the heinous nature of Moens's transgression. Rachel leaned back in her chair and smiled approvingly. Dr Shahak smiled at Rachel and me. It was emotionally a fitting ending to a pleasant dinner.

It took us ten days to get back to the topic. We chose to engage the cooperation of the three in New York. We decided to go back to New York and let them know that we intended to pursue Moens and make sure he didn't start working for the NAACP. While this meant that we'd be going against their decisions, we thought it was worth a try. We figured that denying him his association with the NAACP would also close the door on his attempt to become a Supreme Court justice.

Despite our faint chance of success, we thought that eliminating Moens's stepping stone to the Court was worth trying. We figured that he'd identified the required stepping stone, lied about his eligibility, and used it to get to the next platform. He was never eligible to go to Berea College in the first place, but he'd figured out that Berea was a channel to Harvard. It became clear to us what the trajectory of his plan was: Berea, Harvard, the NAACP, then the Supreme Court.

Dr. Shahak knew of our plans to go back to New York. He called Rachel and asked her if she had the time to meet with another defamation attorney while there. When Rachel asked why that specific attorney, he told her that he knew his father well, a graduate of Yale law, and he had just appeared on *60 Minutes*. He also happened to be very handsome, very successful, and Jewish. Rachel laughed. "Dad, I'll marry a Jew if I happen to love him, and I will marry a non-Jew if I happen to love him. Do you hear me? But if he's willing to have dinner with all of us and provide free legal advice, why not."

Dr. Shahak thought it was a great idea and told Rachel that he had no strong preference for a Jewish contender, and that she could marry a Palestinian so long as she were in love. "Since the only Palestinian I know is Yara, I think it is probably not going to be a Palestinian," she told him. In the end there were eight of us, including the three women in New York, Marvin the attorney, and Jamal, Jameela's brother.

We managed to meet with Marvin in advance of the dinner. We told him to approach the subject gingerly so as not to scare off the New Yorkers. He promised he would. To our surprise and disappointment, Joanne, Summer, and Laticia were very reserved. We sensed that something was wrong when Laticia said that she wasn't sure. When Marvin asked, "Not sure about what?" she answered that she wasn't sure she wanted to get involved. He didn't ask any other questions after that.

As the three New York women were leaving, Marvin tried again by inviting them to join us for an after-dinner drink at his apartment. They declined. We ended up having the after-dinner drink at the same restaurant. Marvin suggested that we not include the three unless they decided they wanted to cooperate. Jameela and Rachel and I were disappointed at their total reversal in attitude. Jameela suggested that someone at Berea must have told Moens, and maybe he'd contacted them and worked his blackmailing magic. Rachel said that if he had gotten the information from Berea, he would have contacted all five complainers about him. She suggested we contact the other two somehow.

I did. Melissa was in Denver and Gladys was in Texas, and Moens hadn't contacted either of them. I took the opportunity to talk to them in a circumspect way about Moens. As the conversation progressed, they both were eager to cooperate as much as they could but, naturally, they didn't volunteer to fly to Massachusetts. I asked them to let me know if Moens tried to contact them in the future, and they sounded willing to oblige.

I shared the news with Rachel and Jameela, and a month later I called Gladys and Melissa again. They hadn't heard from Moens. Rachel was sure that Moens hadn't gotten their names from Berea and that somehow it could have been accidental. Moens could have, by chance, contacted one of the three New Yorkers and gotten the names of the other two from her.

Rachel again asked me to contact the three New Yorkers to see if any of them had given Moens the names of the other two. I did, and each said that he had never asked for the other two names. At that point, it was clear to all three of us that he'd gotten the names in a clandestine way, possibly from us. The first thought that came to mind was that he stole a copy of our telephone bill in Cambridge. But Rachel reminded us that the phone bill was being handled and paid for by her father.

At that point, we had nothing else to analyze; we agreed to think about it. I asked Rachel and Jameela not to frustrate ourselves for fear it would affect our studies. We wanted to avoid making the topic of Moens the only thing we talked about. We agreed not to broach the subject unless there was something new.

Within days, Rachel got a note in the mail. It said: "Don't get involved—it might end up costing you." We all thought that short of Jameela's rape, the note was Moens's most brazen act, and above all, it portended an ominous escalation. Rachel contacted her father, who got very concerned and suggested that the matter needed to be investigated by a private detective. None of us objected.

A week later, the private investigator, Philip, met with all three of us. Philip had been an FBI agent for five years before quitting to pursue a law degree at Columbia. He was supporting himself by taking on side jobs. The first question he asked was whether any of us had told anyone else what was happening with Moens. To our surprise, Jameela confessed that she had shared it with her brother. Philip asked to talk to Jamal face-to-face. Somehow, the suggestion of including Jamal didn't sound like a good idea to me; it involved a third party. Philip said that he would handle it.

He also contacted Marvin to make sure he didn't share anything about Moens with anyone. Marvin was surprised, as he said he never shared his legal activity with anyone except his legal assistant. Philip apologized and told Marvin that was he thought, but he wanted to make sure. Marvin said that he wouldn't touch the subject unless asked in the future. Although Rachel and I thought that Jamal was honest and trustworthy, we didn't know if Jameela had insisted on his full discretion. I proposed that the three of us talk to Jamal. Instead, Philip insisted on calling Jamal himself.

Jamal called Jameela later and told her that Philip was very professional and polite but most inquisitive, and that he did not care to be interrogated, even by a deferential professional like Philip. There were too many questions for Jamal's comfort. Jameela tried to soothe Jamal's feelings, but when he kept arguing with her, I asked for the phone and talked to him. I told him that I sympathized with him but to consider Philip's questions as a necessary annoyance. I then said, "You guys in America are very sensitive to such intrusions. Why do you think I don't want to visit my parents in Amman? The government in reaction to a couple of critical articles in Berea's paper would probably cause me to be interrogated five times as long, and that wouldn't even make me half as sensitive as you were to Philip's questions."

Jamal sounded surprised and didn't argue the point further. He shifted the conversation to my situation. He asked why my parents wouldn't visit me in the States instead of me visiting them in Jordan. I told him that my mother was afraid of flying and that my father had decided years ago not to go anywhere without her. He then asked why my parents wouldn't drive to Syria, so I could meet them in Damascus. "After all, Damascus is barely four hours by car, including the stop at the border crossing," he said. I was impressed that he knew such details. I told him that meeting my parents in Damascus was a plausible alternative. Jamal showing care for my situation felt good, respectful. Or was it more than that? I'd already noticed Jamal's manly and handsome looks, not to mention his intellect.

I wanted to know if Jameela had detected anything. Immediately after I talked with Jamal, I told Jameela, "Nothing works better in soothing somebody's feelings than making him feel his problems are nothing compared to yours. I told him why I'm hesitant to visit Amman, and he was understanding." Jameela responded, "That's why I went back home last month. I wanted to seek Jamal's advice. I hate to brag about my brother, but he's so smart and down to earth." I agreed with her, trying not to reveal my aroused interest in her brother.

Within days Philip was back, and Jamal drove to Cambridge from New York at his request. Philip said that he wanted Jamal there because he needed to impress upon all of us who were in the know how important it was that no one share any information with anyone else. He suspected that Moens had either managed to install an eavesdropping device or tap the house phone. He added that he was surprised that Moens hadn't contacted Amanda and Gladys, despite the fact that their names were mentioned repeatedly at home and over the phone.

Philip then asked us to check our rooms for listening devices. He spent over two hours inspecting the premises through and through, but he couldn't find anything. He then proceeded to see if our phone was tapped. It wasn't tapped in the house, and we couldn't think of anywhere else.

We all accompanied Philip to the garage, where all the house electrical and electronic connections originated and where Rachel and Jameela parked their cars in a doorless garage. In passing, I said that we had discussed meeting the three New Yorkers on our drive to the city. Philip asked us which car we had used for the trip. He proceeded to look through the interior and soon found a recording device underneath Rachel driver's seat.

After he played its contents, he concluded that while it was a blank tape, others might have been retrieved since he had started. It was a noise-activated device that recorded upon opening the door or starting the car. While we knew then the source and mechanisms used by Moens to spy on us, the follow-up steps had to be considered carefully. Philip didn't want any of us to confront Moens. At the same time, he wasn't sure that going to the police was a good idea.

Philip returned the device to where it was, explaining that we didn't want to alert Moens that we were onto him. He said that he needed time to think of a suitable scheme and we agreed to meet the following day. His plan entailed revealing the name of Melissa, ostensibly living in Denver, and giving out her phone number, without mentioning her last name or relating her to Berea. Philip wanted to test how specifically Moens had transgressed against Melissa. By not defining who Melissa was, he wanted to prevent a potential future accusation that we'd used someone without their permission. We waited for Philip to install a specific home set in Denver with a taping mechanism before we mentioned Melissa. The hope was that Moens would then call her to unintentionally reveal his tactics and plans.

Through the help of a Denver private investigator, a phone was set up in his office with a standardized female voice message saying that Melissa was out of town and asking for the name and phone number of the caller and the reason for the call. Moens must have retrieved the tape from Rachel's car and listened to it because, as hoped for, he called the phone number.

The first time, he left his name and phone number. The second time he called, he apologized for his behavior toward her at Berea and mentioned that he'd become a changed man, about to graduate from Harvard Law. He then asked Melissa not to believe me, nor to believe either of my friends. He told Melissa who I was and that I'd resorted to secretly becoming a call girl to help my ailing father in a Palestinian refugee camp.

We all listened to the tape on a conference call arranged by Philip. Jamal was in on the call too. We were all upset, although we shouldn't have been, not after Moens had raped Jameela. I couldn't help myself. I started crying. The description of my refugee status and prostitution hit me hard. I knew that the Palestinians were known for their high social morals. Our refugee status never developed a culture of dereliction, including prostitution or panhandling. Everyone could hear me, including Jamal. He spoke first. "Don't do this to yourself, Yara. He's nothing but a morally and ethically decrepit creature. He's a psychological misfit and doesn't deserve anything less than being in jail for a long time."

Both Rachel and Jameela hugged me, but I couldn't stop crying. Philip asked if we could have another conference call in a couple of days. I told Rachel and Jameela that I needed to go to my room and lie down. Jamal asked me not to be harsh on myself and that if everyone agreed, he could bring along two bottles of French Pauillac wine. Philip said that he'd like to join the group but couldn't make it until the following weekend. Rachel said that we could wait, and not to worry about me, and jokingly said that she had a bottle of Burgundy she could share with me in the meantime.

None of us noticed that Rachel had readily, but sneakily, agreed to postpone our gathering to accommodate Philip's schedule. It sounded very natural, yet it was anything but. It took me few days to get over listening to Moens's description of me. Rachel and Jameela were most kind in trying to comfort me and soothe my feelings.

The gathering took place the next week and included Jamal and Philip. Jamal and I exchanged information about French wines. He not only chose the Pauillac but knew the varieties of wines that went into it, as well as being well informed about wines in general and French wines in particular.

My knowledge of and respect for wine resurfaced my appreciation for the transformation that the Allards had produced in me. After a mere two summers in Paris, I'd changed from a shy and simple teenage girl with a limited horizon to a young woman who appreciated the finer things in life.

Appreciating wine had been one aspect of my transformation. It enhanced my interactions with others, including those with whom I'd had prudent sexual relations. While my relationship with Jean Pierre was unplanned, I'd appreciated it because the pleasure of our experiences was mutual. I thought of him as a young but most considerate lover.

My exchanges with Jamal strengthened my attraction to him—both because of his general knowledge and his concern for me. While I was concentrating on my own feelings, a different dynamic was taking place. Rachel was showing interest in Philip. Neither my interest in Jamal nor Rachel's interest in Philip were apparent to Jameela, and mine wasn't apparent to Rachel either. Both Rachel and I had to concentrate on the purpose of our gathering.

Philip couldn't risk using another voice that Moens could recognize as other than that of the real Melissa. He decided to change the recording, saying that Melissa was in India and didn't have easy access to a phone. She asked the caller to write to her. Moens wrote Melissa his first letter. In it, he repeated his apologies to her for his behavior at Berea and asked Melissa if she could respond to his note.

It wasn't easy. At that point, Philip contacted the real Melissa to check on her attitude toward Moens. She indicated in no uncertain terms that she didn't want to have anything to do with him. That was Philip's opportunity to ask her if she minded him relaying her sentiments to Moens, if and when the opportunity presented itself. She agreed.

Philip got hold of a Pan Am stewardess who accepted the task of dropping a letter to Moens from Bombay. The letter, supposedly from Melissa, thanked Moens for his contact but asked him to let her know if he was willing to apologize for his specific misconduct in writing. Moens answered that he was willing to fly to Denver and apologize to her in person. We all surmised that Moens was too careful to put things in writing; it would have provided additional incriminating details. He was good at placating others in person, provided he could control his emotions.

Nevertheless, we felt good that he was cornered, and in the process had revealed preliminary information that might serve us in the future. In the evening, we went out to dinner and celebrated. Philip took care of the tab, but we knew it was all at Dr. Shahak's expense.

Chapter 12

Throughout Jamal's visit, Jameela was in the best of moods. She looked so proud of her brother, soon to get his PhD in psychology, handsome and very sociable. This time, she insisted on driving him to the airport. She had her arms around his waist on their way to the car, acting giddy. After she started her old and noisy Volkswagen Beetle, she remembered that Rachel kept several Kleenex boxes in her car, and she had none. She got out of her car as she was talking to Jamal. "We're going to get this S.O.B. He has no idea that Rachel's car has much more than Kleenex. It has the tools of his entrapment—his own recording equipment—so be careful saying anything within five feet of it. I don't know when the recorder is on and when it's off."

Little did Jameela or Jamal notice that the noise of the Volkswagen engine had activated Moens's recording device and resulted in recording what Jameela had just said. It took Moens less than a week to retrieve the latest tape, initially to everyone's satisfaction but to our utter disappointment later. Although it was a faint recording, Moens must have figured out the gist of the conversation when he listened to the tape.

Within ten days of Moens retrieving the tape, Jameela got a phone call. It was a similar call to those I'd received earlier. The caller propositioned her and offered to pay $150. He proceeded to tell her how much he enjoyed making love to Black women and that he would be sending a limo to pick her up and for her to choose the date and time.

I wasn't there when the call came. Rachel must have been waiting for my return to tell me in detail what had happened. In addition to what such a humiliating preposition entailed, Jameela felt that it had racist overtones.

Since the call, she'd confined herself to her room. Once more, Rachel heard her crying. I didn't know what to do; this latest news deflated us. When Rachel told me that, my face suddenly drained of color. I asked her for advice, and, in response, she said that she had none. She then said that she needed to consult with her father. I told her not to and that I needed time to think about Moens's latest harassment. Rachel agreed.

I felt empty and confused. Again, I felt I was the cause of all the troubles with Moens, and that such troubles now engulfed everyone, either directly or indirectly but always harshly. Although I didn't mind suffering as a result, I didn't want it to spread to everyone I knew and cared for. I thought about the choices I faced. The following day, I knew what I had to do. I decided to declare defeat.

That morning, I told Rachel that I wanted to talk to everyone at the same time. A meeting was scheduled in the evening for two days later. In the meantime, I contacted the University of Michigan Law School. I asked Rachel not to tell Jamal and Philip what the urgency was all about. Initially, Jameela didn't want to attend the gathering. Rachel told her that the meeting was absolutely crucial and that without it, we could not continue to live together.

I arrived with a cautious but firm presence. My face showed it, yet my eyes were focused and unflinching. I commenced talking in an unusually hushed and serious voice. I could see the smiles disappearing, followed by faces developing a blank expression. There, I apologized to everyone and particularly to Jameela. I told her that I had never caused anyone else more harm in my whole life. She said nothing. She looked at me intently, probing for an elaboration on my statement.

I continued addressing Jameela. "After all I've done to you, I don't deserve to be in your life any longer." She looked at me with a condescending and dismissive demeanor. She held her chin in her left hand, holding back a few anxious tears. I then addressed the group. "I don't know why, but as much as I've tried to be careful, I have impacted your lives in a negative way. My challenge to Moens has taken precious time from each of you, including Dr. Shahak, who wasn't invited to this gathering. I am sure Rachel will relay to him my love and gratitude, for he volunteered his help without even having been asked.

"But the news isn't all grim," I went on. "The University of Michigan Law School has, in the meantime, accepted my transfer, with full credits. Yes, I think it is time to spare all of you the pain caused by my actions. I think it is best to call it quits voluntarily before events force us to do it. After all, seven years ago I never even dreamed of being a law student at Harvard. I am a daughter raised in a refugee camp, and I have already achieved, with everyone's help, a hundred times more than I thought I deserved. In two days, I'll move out to live somewhere else and finish the semester. I know I'll be running into Rachel every day at classes. I think it would be best not to even acknowledge each other. I want to use every opportunity to relay this to Moens. He is evil and determined. I think he is also sharp and opportunistic enough to realize that it is in his best interest not to have permanent enemies."

I stepped toward Jamal and Philip to shake their hands. Philip reciprocated. Jamal pulled back and said, "No, I won't shake your hand, because I don't agree with what you're doing. Moens will not stop. He is a vicious animal, who smells blood. He won't stop until he completely mauls everyone here all the way to the bare bone. On the contrary, declaring defeat will only embolden him; he'll ride high when you leave and challenge himself to harm Rachel and Jameela more than he has harmed you."

Jameela was wiping her tears when Rachel went to the phone and called her father. She was talking with him openly, with the obvious intention of my overhearing the conversation. Philip was saying nothing, as he had no personal relationship with any of us and was only working at the behest of Dr. Shahak. Jamal told me that I was inconsiderate in severing my relationship with everyone. "It's not only inconsiderate but selfish," he said. "You're free to do whatever you want, but remember that when this thing simmers down you will have hurt people who really care for you."

I looked at Jamal disapprovingly and proceeded to go to my room. I sat at the edge of my bed and started crying quietly. It was early in the evening, but not late for me to rest my weary body. The thought of adding one more victim had taken its emotional toll on me. I woke up at four in the morning but stayed in bed, trying to gauge my thoughts and my actions, with little ability to think straight.

At around six in the morning, Rachel knocked on my door to let me know that Dr. Shahak was on the phone. She didn't press the issue and walked back to her room. I hesitated for a while but decided to be polite and talk to him. He was so gracious in the way he described me and my contribution to his family's life, all in flowing terms. I argued back, telling him that while my intentions in confronting Moens were pure and good, the end result was too disappointing, and I didn't want it to involve everyone who was close and dear to me.

I continued to argue that my motives might be altruistic in that I needed to unburden myself of the racial guilt that was bothering me. I told him that the future demanded that I disengage from everyone, as I wouldn't be able to withstand harming any new victims or adding to the harm I had already inflicted on so many, including him. Dr. Shahak asked if he could call me back in the next hour or two. Again, I didn't want to be rude, so I accepted tepidly.

Within half an hour, Dr. Shahak was back on the phone. As soon as I said hello, I could hear Annette's voice. "I'm on a conference call with both of you," she said. "What are you doing, my love? You're abandoning everyone and enrolling at Michigan? What kind of a stupid decision is this? That is not my girl. My girl is a fighter, smart, and not a quitter. Don't worry about the feelings of other adults in this case. They'll tell you directly if they want out. Remember what Robespierre said: 'To punish the oppressors is clemency, to forgive them is cruelty.' You're forgiving Moens and being cruel to yourself and everyone else. I'm not going to repeat what I've just said. You're intelligent enough to know exactly what I'm saying, and I know you'll make the right decision. After all, I am your mother, your French mother, *ma douce fille*." This brought tears to my eyes.

Dr. Shahak asked if I could delay my decision to move out for a week. "If you have any feelings for your family in Pennsylvania, I hope you'll make this small sacrifice," he said. I paused for several seconds, and then agreed. Dr. Shahak then asked to speak to Rachel to let her know that I was staying put for another week. Rachel immediately knocked on Jameela's door and went in to tell her the good news.

The days after my phone conversation with Dr. Shahak and Annette were uncomfortable, as I continued to live with two people I'd intended never to see again. We all spoke in hushed voices and said very little. I couldn't help but feel that I was adding to the discomfort of others, even when there was nothing serious taking place. Neither the days nor the nights passed smoothly. They felt twice as long and totally aimless.

Five days later, I waited for Dr. Shahak to meet me at the house. Rachel and Jameela confined themselves to their rooms, having been alerted to Dr. Shahak's time of arrival. He stepped in but kept the door open. I could feel my anxiety increasing. I heard footsteps, feminine-sounding footsteps. I thought it was Mrs. Shahak, but to my surprise, it was none other than Annette.

She sped toward me and gave me the tightest hug I had ever experienced. She held my head and put it on her shoulder. She then stroked my back gently. Again, she said, "Ma douce fille": my sweet daughter. I looked at her and said, "*Ma douce maman, quelle grand surprise. Je suit sur un nuage*" (My sweet mother, what a surprise. I am on cloud nine).

That was the second time Annette referred to herself as my mother, all in a matter of days. I adored her. I went to my room holding Annette's hand and saying nothing. Dr. Shahak signaled that he was going to Rachel's room. Again, I sat at the edge of the bed, and she sat opposite me. We looked at each other without saying anything. It was a moment that affirmed that the Allards had become as precious as my biological parents were. In one sense, they had something my simpler parents didn't have. Despite my early disjointed circumstances, the Allards and I had developed a harmonious and mutually admiring relationship. Their personalities were the major factor. My improving circumstances and my similarly liberal outlook played a complementary part. Socially, I had picked up something of Annette's style and even her feelings.

I hugged Annette and kissed her on both cheeks. I didn't know what to say. I let go of her hand and signaled that I was heading to Rachel's room. As soon as Rachel opened the door, I hugged her tightly and put my head on her shoulder. Rachel pulled my head back and gave me two kisses, one on each cheek. We didn't have to say anything. We both knew that I had changed my mind.

After our long hug ended, Rachel looked at me and asked, "Do you think I was able to sleep at all last night? You're one of us now. You can't just pack up and leave. Promise me that you won't do this again, and I'll promise you that I'll be at your side all the way. I know Moens is a threat, but he can't defeat us if we stick together and fight back hard."

Rachel grabbed me by the hand and pulled me into Jameela's room. The three of us hugged for a long time. Rachel then asked Annette and her father to come into Jameela's room. She said, "Yara has promised that she won't leave."

At that moment, Annette said, "But nobody has introduced me to Jameela. Yara, what happened to your etiquette?"

As soon as she had the chance, Jameela called Jamal, who was surprised but most delighted at my "coming back to my senses." He told Jameela that he hadn't slept a wink the prior night. Jameela told him that she hadn't either and laughed at this when she told me what Jamal had said. In the evening, we all celebrated at dinner with two bottles of premium French Pauillac, courtesy of Dr. Shahak.

During our dinner, we edged into campaign mode. Dr. Shahak said that, for me to feel better about myself, I needed to lead the group in deciding how and when to proceed, with the help of Philip, Jamal, and the attorney. I was surprised that he included Jamal, but Dr. Shahak explained that he'd consulted him. What I couldn't tell at the time was why Dr. Shahak had considered contacting Jamal in the first place. My conclusion was that he found him intelligent and trustworthy.

Dr. Shahak's suggestion that I should lead the group was music to my ears, as I wanted so badly to defeat Moens and to prove myself to everyone involved that I was worth their grief over my unwise separation plans. I thought that if I could defeat Moens, it would be poetic justice, and that the perpetrator would end up being vanquished and the victim would be the vanquisher.

Chapter 13

For the first time, I felt challenged in a big way. It felt different. This time I wasn't dealing with a transient problem; it was a long process, and possibly an endless process, which also happened to involve a dozen different people, most of whom were precious to me. My feelings toward Jamal were positive, warm, and hopeful, but still undefined. Philip was a close and considerate consultant, with signs of being more, as I sensed a mutual attraction between him and Rachel.

What weighed heavily was the enormity of the challenge, one that needed to be put in proper context, except that the perimeters were continuously expanding. While I felt sanguine about my realization that it was different and more daunting than before, I was hard-pressed to begin formulating a plan to tackle this challenge. Suddenly it came to me. Why not contact my father in Jordan and see if he could come up with a different perspective? I knew he had a lot of horse sense, and he seldom failed when I needed guidance. He might have been challenged about modern liberal issues, but there was nothing new about what Moens was doing. Henry the Eighth had done the same and more.

I thought it was worth it to try. I budgeted forty dollars to have a circumspect conversation with him, speaking in Arabic, and I decided to pretend I was trying to help a friend. I was expecting a long and detailed answer, with many admonitions and provisions. What happened was beyond simple, and unexpected. He paused for a while and said, "I don't know America to any degree, but it's obvious that he won't quit attacking your friend. In this case, she has one avenue: to take the offensive or risk losing the battle."

His answer was revealing. It hit me right away, as if it were the advice of a sage, or even a spiritual revelation by a holy man. I paused and said nothing. My father continued. "Are you with me or not? Can you see what I'm thinking?" I said nothing at first, trying to minimize my ready acceptance of his advice, and then I added, "No, no, I hear you. I'll mention it to Jameela. I'll let her decide for herself." I knew I had found my answer, though I was still in need of a detailed plan. The call was so brief that it only cost four dollars. I promised myself that I'd come up with a complete plan for taking the offensive. I intended to do all the thinking at night while lying in bed.

I approached Rachel and Jameela about resuming our routine dinner plans. I hoped that would be the start of my efforts to get back to normal. That same evening, I went to bed early, hoping to be inspired. I spent over three hours thinking about it, but nothing concrete came to mind. I woke up the next morning disappointed and frustrated and went to class with a headache. Clearly, I needed someone else to help me figure out a plan of action.

I remembered Dr. Shahak mentioning how intelligent and thoughtful Jamal was. That was one potential source of help. But how could I contact Jamal without Jameela knowing about it? I picked up the phone ten times before I ventured dialing. When Jamal answered, he was pleasantly surprised. "To what do I owe this honor?" he asked.

"There's no honor involved; this is a challenge," I said. He laughed, not having the slightest clue about the purpose of my call. "First, you have to promise me that you won't share this with anybody, including Jameela," I said.

"Yara, anything between the two of us won't be shared with anyone else unless you say otherwise," he said. It sounded like he was smiling.

"I want you to tell me what you think about using some of Moens's methods against him," I said. Jamal went silent and then asked me to give him an example. I told him that I was thinking of trying to tape Moens's conversations. Jamal paused again and then asked, "Are you being serious?"

"Yes," I said. "If war is waged against you, you have to wage war against the aggressor, and you may resort to using his tactics, but none worse," I said, trying to rationalize my plans. Jamal told me that an illegal reaction was no more and no less than an illegal action.

I told him that short of taking the war to Moens, there was no other choice but to declare defeat. I reminded him that all along his was the strongest voice urging me to fight back. He begged me not to do anything for the time being and asked if I could meet him in New York sometime during the coming month. I told him that I couldn't wait for a whole month. I added that I could meet him the coming weekend but that I had to come up with an excuse for Rachel and Jameela. We agreed on the details. I was to leave on Saturday and spend the night there, under the guise of meeting a cousin. As an afterthought, I decided to actually contact such cousin to try and validate the cover-up. I had never met my cousin Khalil, despite his attempt to get together years earlier.

I took the train to New York, where I was met that afternoon by Jamal. He insisted on carrying my small suitcase. We stopped as we left the train station. He looked at me and said that I could stay in Midtown or Harlem. He said that he knew of a bed and breakfast where both of us could stay overnight for free. At first I thought he was suggesting we share the same room. He then added that he was more than happy to let me stay in the larger of any two rooms available.

He explained later that he was a member of an NYU Black psychological team, providing free psychological services in the area. The owner of the bed and breakfast was the aunt of one of the patients. Jamal planned to have two sessions with her nephew that weekend. It all sounded OK to me, and I was eager to visit Harlem. When I got there, I was impressed with the B&B. Each level was built around a long gallery, specifically well-lit to exhibit unique, large, colorful artwork on the walls. It turned out that the owner Velma, who was a renowned painter herself, exhibited her work and that of other Black expressionist painters at her small hotel.

When Jamal introduced me to Velma, she gracefully looked me up and down and tipped her head toward Jamal, expressing her approval of my looks. Jamal was quick to say, "Yara is my sister's roommate, and she's here to tour the area. I happen to be her tour guide." He looked at me and then added, "I wish." Velma looked at him and said, "This hotel is one of fulfilled wishes. Ask any artist exhibiting here and they'll tell you their luck changed here in the most unexpected way. What do you say, Yara?"

I smiled and looked at Velma. "Oh god, do I need a change of luck! It's been awful the last few months. This is why I am here to see Jamal. I am told he is a sage of a man." Velma looked at both of us and said, "Well, whoever he was, he must have been awful. I know at least three gorgeous guests who would love to go out with this handsome hulk. You ought to give it a try!"

At that point, I didn't want to play hard to get. I said, "Well, I'm here to seek Jamal's help in getting rid of a chronic problem. His name is Moens, and he isn't, nor has he ever been, a friend. He is surely an enemy."

"You know what they say: To get over one pain, you need to overwhelm it with a substitute—a pleasing substitute," said Velma, winking at me and looking at Jamal.

Jamal asked Velma to stop it. Velma said that she wouldn't stop it and that when the opportunity presented itself, Jamal should act and act fast. "I still have my largest suite available. You two can share it if you would rather not stay in separate rooms," she said. I answered, "Relations should start by closeness of the minds, not by closeness of physical bodies. I think Jamal and I think alike, but we need to come out with the same conclusions," I said. Velma wouldn't let go. "Well, when you come to the same conclusions, let me know. I can make the suite available next time."

Jamal was anxious to change the subject. He said that if I didn't mind, the two of us would have dinner at the hotel, where they served outstanding soul food. I looked at Velma and told her that I was looking forward to it but that I couldn't eat any pork. Velma said, "Oh, you're Jewish. You don't look very Jewish." When I asked what made me not look Jewish, she said nothing, and I could not tell what she meant. I then told her that Muslims, like most Jews, did not eat pork. Jamal interrupted, "I don't eat pork either. Velma knows that but likes to always test the waters." Velma excused herself to let her cook know not to add any bacon to the dish.

That afternoon, Jamal took me on a stroll through Harlem. The two of us were noticed; some of the comments were positive, and others were testy. Many were admonishing Jamal for not going out with a Black girl. Jamal tried to ease my concern and surprise. Some comments were admiring ones, like "Good choice" or "I like Puerto Rico." We ran into a colleague of Jamal's, a sociology instructor at NYU. She was Black and beautiful. She shook hands with me and started speaking with what sounded like fluent Spanish. When I told her that I didn't speak any Spanish, she tried to discern my accent and said, "Wow, Jamal, you're getting adventurous." I told her that not only did Jamal know where I was from, but he could tell the distance from one city and another in Palestine. I clearly wanted to expose her insensitivity.

I felt a little uneasy being the only non–Black person out on the street. I wondered why I felt this way. At the ice cream parlor, another Black customer recognized Jamal. She called him "professor." She happened to be one of his students at NYU. She looked at me and said that Jamal was very popular, not only with Black girls but with white ones too, and that he was popular with his colleagues and his female students. "Like me. You don't mind, do you?" she said. It was clear that I wasn't the only one who found him attractive.

He tried to resume our conversation about my taking the offensive against Moens. I asked him if we could delay discussing that until dinner. When he politely asked why, I told him that our walk was exposing me to Black culture in a very interesting and concentrated way, and I wanted to enjoy the experience. I added that I wanted to react to people. "Then let me take you to one place where they appreciate expressing their opinions and listening to different points of view," he said. He took me to a café, where most people were playing chess. He asked me if I played, and when I told him that I didn't, he proceeded to try and teach me. I balked at first, but he insisted.

We spent three hours together, with Jamal meticulously teaching me chess, step by step. After he identified the different pieces, he showed me the allowed moves for each. Three hours later, I managed to last three to four moves against him. He claimed that I was a quick study. I couldn't tell if that was true or not. All I could tell is that I was enjoying myself and happy that Moens wasn't the subject of our conversation.

After resting in my room, I showered and joined Jamal for dinner. I facetiously apologized for not wearing an evening dress. This I'd learned from Annette. I could see Jamal observing every move of mine. The French had taught me well, and I adapted as if I was meant to have been raised in such a culture. Although we'd had dinner before as part of a group, this time Jamal observed how I handled every sip of my soup and each small morsel of my food. Above all, he could see how I chewed my food and how I swallowed it. It was as if my mouth were a compartment by itself, to open only before my fork went in and after the food was pushed down my throat.

While he was properly mannered, I observed how he talked while some food was still in his mouth. Annette had spent a couple of weeks teaching me how to manipulate my mouth and coordinate its movements in line with what I was doing at the time.

He commented on it, saying, "I'm just curious. Do they eat the same way you're eating now at the refugee camp you were raised in?" I burst out laughing, close to spitting out my food. I said, "You must have forgotten about one important timeline of my life. I spent two summers in France, with very caring and sophisticated surrogate parents. Before then, I only used a spoon to eat, and I'd never used a fork and knife together."

Jamal sighed and said that Jameela had mentioned Annette and Antoine but hadn't given any details. I told him that I'd only shared those details with Rachel and Dr. Shahak. He then asked why I hadn't shared them with Jameela, even though I had been her roommate for eight months. I had to think for a while before I answered. I told Jamal that since I was raised in a refugee camp, my stories almost invariably described how much I had progressed since then. And while Jameela was a most caring person, she looked at me as if I was born with an air of sophistication. "She, on the other hand, seems to feel that her accomplishments aren't readily recognized, and that her Blackness gives others, especially discriminating white people, the opportunity to try to keep her down," I explained.

Jamal paused and looked me in the eye intently. "You're one very perceptive person," he said. "I always thought Jameela was too sensitive. Unlike me. I feel I'm at the same level of anyone, Black or white, and only our ethics or standards separate us. I think you're the same way, cultural differences withstanding." Then he asked if I wanted to go to a top-notch jazz club after dinner, one of the best in the country.

"Do they have premium Margaux or Pauillac?" I asked.

"No, but for you I can buy a very decent Pauillac on the way to the club. I always want to make sure I'm drinking a wine of proven quality," he said. He added that he knew I required a fine wine to enjoy the evening. On the way to the club, Jamal stopped by a liquor store and bought a ten-dollar bottle of Pauillac. I was taken aback, as not even twenty dollars would buy a premium Pauillac. When we got to the jazz club Jamal had his wine in a large paper bag. He ordered a French bottle of table wine. When I asked him if I could look at the wine, he said not to worry. He went to the bathroom and emptied out the bottle from the club and refilled it with the Pauillac.

I then challenged him as to whether what he had done was ethical. He said that it would have been unethical if he hadn't paid the $20 dollars for the club's bottle. I then asked about the $10 Pauillac. He told me that he was in the habit of buying the same wine to take home and that the original price of that Pauillac was $40, but since the label had gotten smeared with wine from broken bottles on the way over to the United States, they were selling it for $10. "So you're drinking premium Pauillac, which arrived in a bottle with a smeared label and was later poured into another bottle of cheap wine."

"How much more exciting can it get?" I asked.

"I think it's all worth it, since I'm doing it all for you," he replied.

I tilted my head, gazing at his face. I asked him what his statement was supposed to mean. He said that it meant whatever I wanted it to. I told him we might as well be talking past each other. He said, "I don't want to force the issue." While I knew well that he was courting me, I said, "What issue?" He tilted his own face and looked at me, smirking, with an inquisitive and dismissive expression.

"If you promise that we'll devote all of tomorrow morning discussing the issue I came down here for, I promise that I'll share with you my understanding of the challenges relative to my situation," I said. He said that he wasn't trying to change anything and that he was well aware that I had a serious topic to discuss, but that the two issues were neither in conflict nor sequential; they existed simultaneously but independent of each other. I told him that I agreed with him and proceeded to give him a soft kiss on his cheek. He looked at me and said, "Does this mean what it's supposed to mean? Getting an answer from you isn't easy. It feels like I'm having a tooth extracted, yet I feel pleasure instead of pain." I told him that his feelings were right on. He smiled again, this time broadly.

The evening went on amiably and warmly. We mostly talked about our backgrounds. I described to him how life was in the refugee camp, how I got to meet the Allards, and how much Annette's nurturing had shaped me and made me into a more mature and modern person. I shared with him that I had a relationship with Jean Pierre at the age of seventeen and that Annette preferred that the relationship not become permanent. "I know now why. She wanted me as a daughter, not as a daughter-in-law, especially since she wasn't sure that the relationship would last."

Jamal told me that his mother was a janitor at a high school when she met his father. She approached him, asking him to help her get a college education. He helped her by tutoring her to prepare for the entrance exam. Two years later, when she went to see him and as he expressed his admiration for her success, she asked him for a date. Both parents were the first in their family to go to college. They got married the day after she graduated.

"You were raised in a refugee camp. My mother was raised by a single mother, free to go anywhere and do so many things, but she might as well have been raised in a refugee camp. She could see and feel the presence of opportunities, but as a Black woman, her choices were very limited. She was gutsy and determined, and my father was considerate and responded to her desires and accommodated her aspirations. Otherwise, she would have been a cleaning lady, just like her mother. I want you to do me a favor. Stop referring to your refugee camp, unless it's necessary. You should watch yourself eating, sipping wine, or talking to Annette in French. You're educated, confident, and sophisticated. Do you hear me, Yara?"

"I hear you loud and clear," I said. "I need to think about all these accolades alone and figure out if they are real; I do my best thinking in bed."

"You're insulting me, Yara. Do you hear yourself? You're saying I'm praising you just to sleep with you."

I stood up and raised my voice. "No, you're misconstruing my statement. I always think things over in bed—everything. It has nothing to do with sex. Why does everyone in America relate everything to sex? I hate it." Jamal apologized and seemed to appreciate my explanation.

Suddenly, it popped into my mind that I'd never called my cousin. It was already 9:30 in the evening; I was hesitant to call him that late. Jamal told me to just go ahead, as 9:30 was still early for New Yorkers. I excused myself to use a phone. Khalil answered. I was afraid he would be cool toward me since I'd never called him back years earlier. When I told him who I was, he was surprised but most welcoming.

When he learned I was in New York, he insisted on seeing me. I was planning to head back to Boston the following day, at noon. Khalil said that he would be available anytime I was available. I didn't know what to say. He then told me that he did a lot of business out of Boston and for me not to worry about my return back, that he'd drive me. We agreed to meet for lunch.

Chapter 14

I told Jamal about connecting with my cousin. We decided to meet in the morning for breakfast to continue our discussions. The weather was ideal. The restaurant we chose had a sidewalk café, where we sat watching a rainbow of passersby.

I approached him crisply so as not to give him a chance to stand up. I was in a joyful mood. With a buoyant smile on my face, I gave him a kiss on his cheek. That seemed to make his morning. I put my hand over his and said, "It's time to be serious. Let me tell you again what I am thinking. In short, I want to take the fight to Moens. I don't think we can play dead or meek, or he'll walk all over us before he applies the final blow."

Jamal agreed with me about taking the offensive but was concerned that my actions would lead to my expulsion from Harvard. I told him that if he genuinely agreed with me and supported my efforts openly, I wouldn't take any action before sharing everything about my plans with Rachel and Jameela. "I want to give them a chance to either be on board enthusiastically or disagree with me and refrain from participating," I said. I explained to him that I was averse to gray situations, and that since no one had accepted my choice of declaring defeat, I had no other option but to seek victory and opt to be on the offensive, regardless of the risks.

Jamal was hard-pressed to give me an answer. He finally said that he'd let me know what he thought in person the following weekend. He added that if he were to decide to support me, then it would be easier to argue my case to both Rachel and Jameela. "I don't want my feelings for you to cloud my decision. I insist on only sharing with you my genuine thoughts; nothing superficial or in response to the needs of the moment," he said. I agreed and thanked him for being so open and honest. I told him that I was looking forward to seeing him, regardless of his decision.

Before he left, he gave me a kiss on my cheek. I liked it and looked at him with a receptive smile. I went back to my room to do some reading before meeting with Khalil. I arrived at the restaurant ten minutes early. I thought I'd recognize Khalil on the spot, imagining that he would look like my other relatives in Amman.

To my utter surprise, Khalil was standing opposite me, and looking straight into my eyes. I hadn't noticed him approaching. It was obvious why I didn't notice him: He was Black. I had been expecting a Middle Eastern person with a Shaheen profile. I hesitated at first, but when he greeted me in Arabic, I recognized him. He was well-built, very tall—over six feet—and handsome, with a lovely, broad smile. I guessed his age to be around thirty-five. As I stood up, he hugged me, and I hugged him back. "Aren't you ashamed of yourself?" he joked. "You've been in this country seven years and waited until now for us to get together." I did feel embarrassed and rather inconsiderate, especially after seeing how impressive and sophisticated he was.

I had totally forgotten that his mother was a Haitian Black

woman, and I should have at least considered that he or his two brothers would be Black. After my half uncle met his mother and married her, he moved to Haiti and lived there for fifteen years, where he made most of his money owning several art galleries. He then moved back to New York City. Khalil was a very successful businessman, supplying half of the medical equipment imported by Haiti. He told me that he had practiced law in New York City before becoming a businessman. He spoke fluent English, Arabic, French, and the local Creole of Haiti. He'd gotten his law degree from the Sorbonne, in France.

It was a most enjoyable lunch. I was beside myself and regretful that I hadn't met him earlier. Two hours later, we proceeded to Cambridge in his fancy Mercedes. Due to his schedule and mine, there wouldn't be any time to visit the following day. We talked a lot on the way, and he promised to come and visit in a couple of months.

On the drive, I was thinking of the best way to approach Rachel and Jameela about my decision. I was seeking honest answers, based on a strong commitment to take the offensive. I needed to present my plan in an unvarnished fashion. I decided that I had to give them every opportunity to turn me down, but first I needed to hear from Jamal. The following Wednesday, he called me early in the morning. He told me that he'd thought about it long and hard and decided that I had no choice but to take the fight to Moens in a determined fashion—even if that meant using questionable tactics. It was a great relief. I didn't want to continue massaging a lie about going to New York to see my cousin. I wanted to be able to say that I was going to seek Jamal's advice and help.

Jamal added that, while he came to his decision objectively, he wouldn't have gotten involved were it not for his feelings toward me. I again thanked him for his honesty and told him, tongue in cheek, that in my case, I appreciated his offer of help and that I was glad he'd reached a firm decision. "Are you kidding me? How many times have I implied and expressed how I feel?" he asked. I then asked him if he still wanted to mention my decision to Rachel and Jameela and if he wanted to let them know that we'd seen each other over the weekend.

We agreed that I needed to let them know that consulting with Jamal was the main objective of my trip. We also agreed that I would present my case and he'd express his support later, after Rachel and Jameela were given a chance to say yes or no. The following Saturday, Jamal drove to Boston, after letting Jameela know about his visit. I could see it on Jameela's face: She was curious about Jamal visiting so often. I made sure that Rachel was at the house. As soon as Jamal arrived and hugged Jameela, I called for Rachel to come out of her room. As we sat in the living room, I told everyone that I needed to share with them several important pieces of information.

"You need to know that the primary objective of visiting New York wasn't to see my cousin but to consult with Jamal," I began by saying. "I've decided to take the fight to Moens and not to wait for him to terrorize any of us further. Jamal and I discussed this at length. My approach isn't going to concentrate on defending myself but on collecting damaging information on him. Instead of reacting to his taping my conversations, I plan to tape his!"

Jameela said that she wanted to hear what Jamal had to say.

Jamal stood up and said that the reason he supported my idea was because I had no choice. He added that he was very much aware of the risks I was facing, and anyone else who would support me would be taking similar risks. He mentioned dismissal from Harvard as one of them. He asked Rachel and Jameela not to support me only out of their strong feelings of friendship. "You should support Yara only if you appreciate and are willing to face such risks," he said.

Jameela looked at Jamal and said half jokingly, "What has this Palestinian done to you? You sound like her lover or her attorney. I thought you were much more cautious than that!" Jamal gave a general answer. He asked Jameela and Rachel to take their time and decide and told them that regardless, he had already made up his mind to support my decision and be involved. Jameela looked surprised at his resolve.

Jamal proposed that we order pizza for the evening, to be accompanied by some fine wine. I was watching Rachel and Jameela. I couldn't tell if their facial expressions were those of surprise or reflected the need to think seriously. Rachel said that she agreed with Jamal on one thing: "This requires careful consideration."

I wanted to make myself scarce so that my new closeness to Jamal wouldn't be detected. I said that pizza was fine with me and that I'd return from campus around six. I wanted Jamal to have his chance to elaborate on his support. Jamal told me later that Rachel and Jameela bombarded him with questions. Jamal explained that his PhD studies were ending in six weeks, so any potential trouble from NYU wasn't a factor, but he expressed his concern for all of us. Rachel and I had two years to go at Harvard, and Jameela had one.

Being his sister, Jameela was merciless. She told Jamal that their parents had sacrificed a lot, sending two Black students to Harvard and NYU. She reminded him that ever since she enrolled at Harvard, their parents seldom ate out. They'd just started to recently, since Jamal was started teaching at NYU. "They'll be devastated if anything happens to jeopardize my graduating from Harvard," Jameela said. "Have you thought of that?"

Jamal nodded. "Yes, I have. I plan to discuss it with them, and if they happen to strongly oppose my participation, I won't go through with it. I don't know how I'd let Yara down if that's the case. I know she'd be seriously disappointed, but I also know that she'll go through with her plans regardless."

Jameela waited for Rachel to go to the bathroom before she grabbed Jamal's arm and asked, "She'll be devastated because of your change of mind, or because you'd be breaking the heart of a beautiful refugee?" Jamal looked at Jameela with bulging eyes and said, "Stop calling her a refugee, beautiful or not. Would you like someone to call you a beautiful Black? It's the same when you call her a refugee." They were talking so loudly that Rachel could hear all the conversation from the bathroom.

When I returned, Rachel was waiting for me outside the house. She took me by the arm into the garage and repeated what she'd heard. I was somewhat disappointed that Jamal's support was facing serious doubts and challenges. After listening to Rachel, I decided to let Jamal know that he could withdraw his support any time. Rachel said, "But I'm with you all the way. I don't care. I'll graduate from another law school, if the situation escalates to that point." I asked her if she was sure. She answered, "I am 100 percent sure. I just want my father's support. I'm also sure he'd support us all the way." I hugged Rachel and then kissed her on her forehead.

We went into the house. Rachel talked to Jamal and Jameela. Jamal was fixing salad. She told them that she'd overheard them arguing and that she told me everything. "I had to, because I happen to support Yara 100 percent, and I want to be involved in this effort." I then addressed Jamal and said that he didn't have to stick to his promise of help; I understood that his parents' situation was very sensitive and that it, of course, had priority over any other consideration.

Jamal said that he wouldn't abandon me unless his parents' objections were adamant. He didn't want the situation to impact their health. I wholeheartedly agreed with him. Suddenly, he said, "You know, Yara, I wouldn't abandon you. You are special to me." Jameela looked at Rachel and Rachel at Jameela. Jameela looked at Jamal and said, "Well, then you might as well take Yara to meet our parents. You don't need to say anything else." Rachel walked toward me and stood beside me without saying anything. She whispered in my ear, "Moens isn't all evil, after all, if he has produced this relationship with Jamal! He's very handsome, and more considerate than Jameela."

"OK, Jameela. I'll ask Yara to come and explain her case directly. I think she could make all the difference," said Jamal.

"Oh, don't play games with me," Jameela said. "You want to introduce Yara to them as your girlfriend or potential girlfriend. Get off it. I know you two have feelings for each other. Neither of you can hide it. You gave yourself away and guess what? I'm thrilled." Jameela ran toward me and hugged me tightly. She told me that she'd never anticipated that this would take place and now that it had, she was beside herself. Then she asked me if I didn't mind if she came along with us to see her parents.

I hadn't said yes to the whole idea, since I wanted to be alone with Jamal. Rachel then said that she also would like to accompany us. "I think when the Armstrongs also hear how much another roommate supports the idea, they'll be more likely to accept our plans," said Rachel. She then whispered in my ear, "When they see you, they'll have no choice."

We all sat down to have our pizza and wine. None of us wanted to continue discussing the plan or my new relationship with Jamal. We talked mostly about the first year of law school finishing in two weeks. Since Rachel and Jameela had mentioned their parents, I said that I wanted to check with the Allards. I told everyone at the table that my real parents, especially my father, would give me the usual generic answers as he had in the past. I thought that my mother would only admonish me not to get in trouble.

We agreed to hunker down until the school year was over. We were all nervous that Moens would do something to disrupt our plan in the meantime. Fortunately, nothing happened. We learned that as soon as the school year was over, Moens left for Kentucky. A few days after both Harvard and NYU ended their semesters, we left to rendezvous with Jamal in New York and then continue to New Jersey. I wasn't sure how Jamal was supposed to introduce me to his parents. When we got to his parents' house, Jamal reintroduced Rachel and then me. They remembered us from when we'd met them months earlier when we came to fetch Jameela.

Jameela kept looking at Jamal as if to ask why he hadn't introduced me as his girlfriend. When I noticed her tense demeanor, I told her that I was looking forward to getting to know her parents and for her parents to know me better. But Jameela seemed restless and anxious, and I couldn't tell why. She asked her mother, Joyce, if she thought I was beautiful. I got mad and tried to change the subject by saying that we were there to celebrate the successful end of the school year, and nothing more. Joyce looked at me and said, "I wasn't born yesterday, I think there's something going on. Will someone tell me what?" I told Joyce that we were there to seek advice from her and Mr. Armstrong. Joyce said that she was old enough to be addressed formally, but she and her husband preferred to be called by their first names. I told her that I would and that I would discuss the subject of our trip at dinner.

As the six of us sat at the dinner table, I got right to the main subject in the hope of having a brief discussion, as I could see everyone felt anxious and wanted to get this over with. I started by emphasizing that I had started the problem and that everyone else could withdraw without any hard feelings. I summarized that Moens was a calculating and vicious person who had his eyes on serving on the Supreme Court, but in the meantime, he was shortly to start working for the NAACP. When Ben Armstrong asked what was wrong with that, I told him, trying to avoid the subject of rape, that Moens might be a self-hating Black who did not relate to his own race and worked against the interest of Black people. He didn't espouse any of the objectives of the organization he worked for, the NAACP. He even refrained from dating Black girls.

Neither Ben nor Joyce could understand why someone like Moens would resort to such a scheme. I was thinking out loud and told them that his father was Icelandic, and perhaps he wanted to look more like his father and not like his mother. I continued by saying that Moens had been on the attack against us for months, publicly accusing me of resorting to selling my body to help out my parents. I added that Jameela and Jamal were there to seek their advice as well, since I'd reached the initial decision to take the offensive on my own.

Both Joyce and Ben paused before Joyce spoke. "If you strongly believe in what you're doing and find it to be the only way, you should follow your better judgment. As for Jameela and Jamal, we helped them get educated and to think for themselves. They don't need our permission to get involved. If they join you in your efforts, they will have our support. They'll have it, too, if they decide not to join you." I told them that the offensive would include taping Moens's phone.

Joyce told me not to share any details with her. When I saw that they were not alarmed about the whole thing, I said, "If we get caught, we could get kicked out of Harvard." Joyce and Ben looked at each other. Ben said, "Harvard isn't the kingdom of heaven. If this is the only way, then it's the only way." I looked around the table to see that everyone appeared to be pleasantly surprised.

But not Jameela. She suddenly said, "Dad, this could even tarnish Jamal's reputation. He's involved, and he seems to be in love with Yara, and if things go bad it could ruin their relationship." While this was plausible, I thought Jameela was trying hard to make her point, using a roundabout connection. I was surprised that Jameela was bringing this up.

Joyce looked at Jameela and said, "You're afraid that what happened to you could happen to your brother." Jameela tried to interrupt, but Joyce continued. "You have to remember that not everyone is alike. I don't think Yara is like Andrew, who dropped you after he thought you were pregnant. I have good feelings about Yara. She isn't American; she's an Arab. Do you know that we named your brother and you after Jamal Abdul-Nasser, the late president of Egypt?" Jameela was actually the female namesake of Jameel, but I wasn't about to correct her. And the names were cousins, derived from the Arabic noun meaning *beauty*.

Joyce's revelation explained why Jameela didn't seem to want to figure me out as an individual. She wanted to lump me in with every other white person who happened to have had a sour romantic relationship with a Black person. Jameela left the table, huffing and in a tizzy. All of us were silent, including Ben and Jamal.

Joyce turned to me to explain. "I think that Jameela is afraid Jamal might be successful where she wasn't. She knew that I liked Andrew, and I'm not certain it was his doing; I think neither one of them really knew how to handle the situation. They fell in love in their senior year in high school and were harassed for it. His father came over to visit. He was considerate and polite, but his mother, excuse my language, was white trash. Joyce continued. "Jamal told me that Yara was raised in a refugee camp. Although challenged, she was lucky. She wasn't treated any differently from anyone else. We Blacks are in a refugee camp called the United States of America. Don't mind this talk about me and Ben having a heart attack if you don't graduate from Harvard. It is all in Jameela's head."

Jamal said, "I knew that Jameela was raising the issue not to influence me but to influence Yara. She probably wasn't a happy camper driving with us this morning. But it seems clear that it's now up to Yara and Annette, and Rachel and Dr. Shahak. It would be nice if we had all the parents on board."

Joyce turned to me and said, "Look at you, smiling. You're lighting up this room. And look at you, having wonderful friends—a Jewish friend and a Black friend; excuse me, two Black friends. I forgot about Jameela." Joyce then laughed with great joy. Ben told her not to rub it in and that Jameela would come to her senses. He looked at me and said, "Go for it. Don't mind anybody else, including your parents and Rachel's parents. You have our blessing." Their sentiment could not have been clearer or more positive. Jamal said that he knew all along that his parents would support my efforts.

Joyce and Ben couldn't have been more hospitable. They insisted that Rachel and I spend the night at their house. Buttressed by their support, Rachel, Jamal, and I left the following morning for Pennsylvania, to meet with Joseph and Sara Shahak. Dr. Shahak was cheerful and welcoming, as always. Sara was as well, but there was less cheer in her demeanor. It was different this time, with Jamal involved. We knew that Dr. Shahak thought highly of Jamal. When Sara met him, I could see the surprise on her face. Rachel was caught teasing Jamal, and Sara might have misconstrued that the relationship was between Jamal and Rachel.

Within a couple of minutes, Sara managed to take Rachel to the side. As she and Sara got back, I could see the smile on Sara's face. Rachel got close to me and whispered that her mother was more religious than her father. I knew what she meant. What I didn't know was whether she objected to Jamal because he was Black or because he wasn't Jewish. I wanted to test the water. Out of nowhere, I approached the Shahaks and said, "It's interesting, because in the Middle East Jamal would be considered white. Here in the US, he's Black." Dr. Shahak jumped at the opportunity to answer. I could tell that he didn't want Sara to upstage him and say the wrong thing. "Well, America isn't proud of its race relations. The Jews and the Arabs are more accepting." I looked at him and said, "I know. We both know that although the Arabs did practice slavery in the past, for the most part it wasn't racial; it was mostly exploitive, and they would have enslaved whites if it were profitable—nothing to be proud of."

Jamal jumped into the conversation. "In the case of Arabs, you can blame it on the free enterprise system."

"I agree, but the system can't act on its own," Dr. Shahak said. "It needs people to perpetrate its evil edicts." He seemed to approve of my stand, as I didn't try to absolve the Arabs of their misdeeds. He added, "We Jews have our own transgressions, more about sex and outsiders—*goyim*—than race. We're all responsible for our current actions. Today's Greeks can't hide behind the accomplishments of their thinkers either; they must account for their current and ongoing behavior. Similarly, the Jews and the Arabs and every other group can be chronicled for their past misdeeds but as individuals can be judged on what they do now."

I took the initiative and told everyone that our visit had a specific purpose, and that Rachel must have shared it with the Shahaks. Dr. Shahak said that Rachel had already told him and asked him to explain where he stood. Dr. Shahak expressed his full support and appeared relieved when Sara didn't object to anything he said.

I was equally determined to be straightforward with the Shahaks, just as I'd been with the Armstrongs. I started by saying that my decision was mine and mine alone and that I'd go through with it even if Rachel, Jameela, and Jamal decided not to join forces. I also said that their lack of participation would have no effect on our relationships whatsoever. Dr. Shahak said that he understood why I'd decided to take the initiative with full force. "But you need to be more specific, Yara! What is your exact plan? How are you going to execute it, and how are you going to pay for it?" I told everyone that I had thought carefully about what Dr. Shahak was asking and that I intended to have a full outline of my plan before I started doing anything.

"The plan won't work unless I get financial support," I said, "which will have to come from my French parents." I could see the relief on Jamal's and Rachel's faces. Dr. Shahak said that he was pleased I was realistic enough to have thought of the financial aspect. He then added, "I hope you don't mind, but I'd like to help too. I'll pay for Philip's services full time for six months."

I put my hands over my mouth and teared up. Jamal had a broad smile on his face. Rachel hugged me and gave me a kiss on my cheek. Dr. Shahak looked at me and said, "But I have one condition." Rachel suddenly looked concerned. "From now on, you have to refer to me and Sara by our first names—and consider us your Pennsylvania parents."

I couldn't help myself; I choked up and started shedding tears and sniffling. Rachel gave me a tissue and then hugged me again while she teared up. Jamal shook hands with Dr. Shahak and nodded his head approvingly several times without saying anything. Then Dr. Shahak ushered us into the kitchen to eat.

Chapter 15

As we sat down to eat, Dr. Shahak looked at me and asked if I had spoken to Antoine or Annette. When I said that I hadn't, but was planning to give them a call, he said that he'd spoken to Annette and that she didn't want to share her thoughts with anyone else before she talked with me. He added that they had agreed, due to the seriousness of the matter, that it would be best if I spoke with Annette and Antoine in person. "Annette accepted my offer to split the price of the ticket to Paris. She also said that you don't need to go back to your house in Cambridge and that she'll have a couple of dresses ready for you, and later you'll spend time shopping together."

Rachel looked at me and said, "I need to go with Yara. I'd like to buy a few Parisian outfits myself. Dad said that it was all up to you." When I wondered why it was up to me, Dr. Shahak said, "If you don't want Rachel to accompany you, I won't buy her the ticket, but Annette was generous enough to also invite Rachel. She didn't say anything about Jameela. I know that next time, Jameela would want to accompany the two of you." I saw that Rachel was as pleased as I was, and Jamal was smiling agreeably.

Before dinner, I asked everyone if they were ready to discuss our plans in detail. Dr. Shahak said that we should wait for Philip, who was joining us. "I'm 100 percent convinced of your general approach, but I think it will be prudent to give Philip the chance to propose a detailed plan," Dr. Shahak said. "Yara, you can let him know what you want to do, and he can figure out how."

Jamal leaned over toward me and whispered in my ear, "There are the legal and liability aspects, too. Philip knows more about them than we do and knows how to maneuver in order not to violate the law." I nodded my head, and so did Rachel.

When Philip showed up to dinner, Rachel had dolled herself up. I wondered if anything had already happened between the two of them. Could Rachel and Philip have gotten together without letting me and Jameela know? I observed the two of them closely. Philip didn't show any particular affection toward Rachel, nor did she toward him. He was semiformal with everyone. But as I continued watching the two, my suspicions were confirmed. I was pretty sure there was a relationship of sorts going on. I saw him slip a note into her hand; Rachel noticed that I saw.

I sat opposite Jamal and Rachel, who was sitting next to Philip. Jamal must have wondered. I planned to explain my change of seat later, but above all, I wanted Rachel to acknowledge that she knew I knew. As we were eating, the Shahaks' cat came to me, seeking attention. I took the opportunity to say, "Some cats are dying for attention and others pretend no one is noticing them, but actually they know they are being noticed but don't want to admit it." Rachel looked at me and said, "No, they all like to admit to it, but they wait for the right opportunity."

After dinner, Rachel took me to the side and told me it was her mother she was keeping this from, not anyone else. She added, "My father genuinely wants you to utilize Philip's services—and so do I, for more than one reason. Philip will be driving to spend every weekend in Cambridge." I thanked Rachel for coming clean and told her that we should talk about it in more detail while we were in Paris.

Two days later, we were on our way to Paris in a new Boeing 747. After we finished inspecting this new and breathtaking plane, we began our discussion of things we had put off until this flight. Rachel told me that when I was in New York visiting Jamal and Khalil, she had called Philip and had him drive over, and they had spent the weekend together. She admitted that the relationship had started right after Philip's first visit. Rachel had called Philip afterward and carefully let out her feelings for him; he had reciprocated by confirming his same feelings for her. It was clearly strong for both of them from the start and must not have needed a warm-up stage.

Rachel asked about me and Jamal. I told her that I liked him a lot and that he presented the perfect opportunity. I added that his race didn't pose a test of any sorts and that the feelings were mutual. When Rachel asked why I wasn't more forward with the relationship, I told her I was concerned that he might not have the same feelings for me, and if there was a breakup, I'd be heartbroken. "With Moens, I was only there to sample having a relationship with a Black man. With Jamal, it could be the real thing," I said.

Rachel told me that I wasn't like her: She could only think of a boyfriend/girlfriend relationship for the time being, and she was leaving the future to chance. At any rate, she was as happy for me as I was for her. I asked her if on this trip we should confine ourselves to shopping and reevaluating what to do about Moens while in Paris.

We started early and discussed Moens all through the seven-hour flight to Paris.

I suggested that we share everything with Annette that we had discussed on the flight. Rachel said that it was a great idea, as discussions of this kind tended to make people closer to each other; in this case, she wanted to get close to the Allards. At the airport, we were met by Annette, Antoine, Jean Pierre, and his fiancée Josephine. Jean Pierre had matured and looked more handsome. When Rachel saw him, knowing he was the one who started my sexual activities, she told me that I was lucky to have such a young and handsome man deflower me. When I jokingly said that I practically deflowered myself, she said that she'd lost her virginity at the age of fifteen.

The Allards were most welcoming to Rachel and showed their customary warmth toward me. Jean Pierre referred to me as his sister. The following morning, Annette took us to her neighborhood café. There, I started by telling Annette how the Shahaks also wanted to adopt me. I wanted to make sure Annette didn't feel used, as if I was jumping from one close, affectionate parental relationship to another. She immediately said, "Why not? If I could, I would have ten sets of parents. After all, you are precious and they are deserving, as we have been." I hugged Annette and told her how kind and generous she had been.

Annette smiled. "This is in the past; now you come from Paris! I'm sure the Shahaks want to adopt you for the same reason we have. Don't sell yourself short, but never get full of yourself, like many Parisians have. But let's not discuss anything serious today; this is a day for shopping."

Our morning coffee lasted two hours. I was wearing one of the two beautiful dresses Annette had had ready for me. When we went to the same store where Annette had bought them, she insisted on buying two similar dresses for Rachel. She then told her that she was going to buy me four or five more outfits, and Rachel could choose and buy some for herself. Before the day was over, we'd visited nine different stores.

The evening was spent at home, where Annette and Rachel got to know each other better. I mostly listened to their conversation. The following morning, we met at the executive offices of the large hotel. Annette told me that the floor was mine, and that she would be taking notes and asking questions later. I got off to a very slow start, almost stuttering at times. It was partly because I was having difficulty coordinating my choices, and now I was talking to Annette and Rachel at the same time. I'd told Rachel almost everything, and I'd shared some details with Annette, but not all. What I'd kept from each was different. I decided that to be open with both was easier and more honest.

I alluded to past times, like a typical French woman, by confirming to Annette that Jean Pierre and I did have a brief sexual relationship. I also told her that my first serious contact with Moens took place for the sole purpose of dating someone from a different culture. With those out of the way, I told Annette that anything else I might have kept from her was minor compared to what I'd just revealed. Annette looked at me and said, "You've done nothing wrong. In both instances, you behaved according to your age. Many people your age have relationships; some are puritanical, and others are sexual. As for this Moens, you had matured and wanted to test your liberalism. It happens all the time. At least you didn't do like many French men do: getting married while knowing that they have no intention of letting any of their other girlfriends go."

I was relieved. I never thought I'd be so flustered in the combined presence of Annette and Rachel. I told her that Dr. Shahak had already hired Philip to do all the clandestine work. Then I told Annette that Philip and Rachel had a relationship and that Dr. Shahak knew about it and encouraged it, as he respected Philip a lot, but that Sara was in the dark.

As for Moens, I described him as a diabolical person who didn't mind using anything and everything once he construed someone as an enemy or potential enemy. "If he doesn't have real ammunition against you, he'll fabricate something," I said. I told Annette how Moens had told people that Jameela and I were carrying out prostitution activities on the side. I then explained how I suspected that his admission to Berea had been dishonest.

"He managed to be hired by the NAACP to defend Black causes, but he continues to be indignant about and dismissive of all Black aspirations, and instead he only desires to oppose and defeat Black efforts, per his own admission." I told her that his ultimate objective was to become a Supreme Court justice, something almost impossible to achieve, but that he'd already managed to fool the NAACP into hiring him. Clearly, he planned to continue deceiving them into recommending him to a position on the Supreme Court.

"My plan is to do anything and everything, short of harming him physically, to expose him. This would include using other men or women to entrap him, taping his conversations, in person or over the phone, and exposing his duplicity to liberal and civil rights–minded professors, if and when I can manage it. I also want to secure copies of his tax returns. I suspect that he was concealing what he was receiving from his father. I'm thinking of other means, too, but this should give you an idea."

Annette looked at me and said, "Listen, Yara. Our experience in Algeria still haunts us. We should have done something, and we didn't. We, the French, acted like animals there, with no respect for the local population. I want you to fight for what you believe in. Dr. Shahak appointed an ex-FBI agent to help you out, and we're going to assign a first-class attorney to advise and defend you, if need be. We've also talked to a top-notch Harvard law professor on your behalf."

When Annette mentioned the name Faintheart, Rachel and I couldn't believe it: He was our favorite professor. Although he taught us a different subject, he was known for teaching torte and especially civil rights torte. When I asked Annette how she had chosen this specific attorney, she told me that he had been recommended by the same American cultural attaché who'd gotten me into Berea.

I hugged Annette, knowing that with her coming on board, she joined the Armstrongs and the Shahaks in supporting my plan. I looked at Annette and said, "Mama, I think we should celebrate and take Rachel where I ate some of the best sweetbread in Paris." When Rachel said that she didn't eat sweetbread, Annette answered that the top chef at the big hotel was working that evening and that he'd cook anything else Rachel wanted.

I thought that the evening would go well, and it did; it was marvelous. Antoine entertained Rachel all evening long while I teased Jean Pierre and sided with his fiancée. Annette observed and enjoyed the gathering while sipping on an exquisite Gevrey-Chambertin. Rachel called Philip and told him how much fun she was having in Paris. She described to him the dresses she had gotten as a present from Annette and the ones she had bought for herself.

They agreed to spend the following weekend together. I decided also to call Jamal, to inform him that my French parents were supporting us 100 percent. He told me that he'd spoken with Jameela and that she had simmered down and promised to help as much as she could.

Chapter 16

Rachel and I couldn't believe how things had fallen into place. The flight from Paris back to New York felt so short, and we talked the entire time. With all the potential measures we had discussed enacting against Moens, I became slightly concerned that our efforts might end up costing much more than any anticipated budget. Rachel eased my concerns, emphasizing that her father and Philip knew how to carry out such measures at bargain prices.

Philip called for a meeting, which also included Jameela, me, Rachel, and Jamal. Rachel and I were most animated. We immediately started talking about shadowing Moens and tapping his phone. Philip stopped us and said that he wouldn't involve himself in anything illegal, which meant that most of our suggestions were off limits. He proceeded to limit the effort to watching, but not shadowing, Moens. He then reminded us that we didn't know much about Moens's habits: nothing about whom he dated, where he ate, how he got to school. Philip said that this information needed to be secured from his family and friends, old and new, and from his other contacts. He didn't want any of us to harass or attempt to intimidate Moens.

When I asked Philip if he expected us to secure the names of Moens's friends and family he said no, that was why he was involved. I didn't want to say anything more but wasn't happy with the severe limits Philip placed on our potential measures. Without sharing my concerns with Rachel, I tried to think of something to do. For several days I couldn't come up with anything concrete.

My deflated feelings didn't escape Rachel's notice. She was keen that I not lose hope. To raise my spirits, she shared with me information she was supposed to keep to herself: namely, that her father was going to reach out to the NAACP and attempt to alert them to the potential danger of having hired Moens.

This news raised my hopes, but unfortunately, two days later, Rachel told me that the NAACP had been less than receptive.

A few days into feeling disheartened, I saw an announcement about the reverend of a local Black church giving a speech at Harvard. It was part of Harvard's community outreach program. I decided to listen to the Reverend, Don Pfeifer. I said nothing about my plans to Rachel or Jameela.

I thought hard about what to say and what to do to possibly involve this church or any Black institution in my cause. I rationalized that since Moens was Black and held a high position with the most active Black organization, I needed to discover or devise something provable and helpful to unmask Moens. Then I wondered if inviting my Black cousin Khalil to accompany me might make a difference.

I called Khalil and presented my case to him. I didn't want him to feel I was using him, so I wanted to make sure that he understood every nuance of my strategy, motives, and tactics. Forty-five minutes into the conversation, Khalil said, "You really didn't need to go into such detail! I'm your cousin, and I'll help whenever I can."

With that statement, he sent me back five thousand miles, all the way to the Middle East. I recalled a popular saying: "My brother and I against my cousin, and my cousin and I against the outsider." When Khalil agreed to come to the presentation, I was grateful to this cousin I hadn't even met until a month ago.

I was feeling good after having been so constrained by Philip. Now I needed to choose a line of potential questions for Reverend Pfeifer. I knew I might get to ask only a couple of questions, if called upon. Something else came to mind. Since I'd never mentioned to Rachel, Jameela, or Jamal that my cousin was Black, why not invite all three to the presentation and take the opportunity to introduce my cousin to them and see what kind of reaction I would get?

I arranged for Khalil to come to our place first. When he rang the doorbell, I made sure I answered the door. I welcomed Khalil in Arabic and invited him in. As soon as he stepped in, I grabbed him by his waist and led him into the living room, where Rachel, Jameela, and Jamal were sipping wine. They all looked surprised, Jamal in particular. I realized that he might think that Khalil was another contender for my affections.

I said nothing at first, and then took my arms off Khalil's waist and said, "This is my New York cousin, Khalil." Their expressions changed from surprise to relief. I said nothing and observed Jamal snap out of it and reciprocate Khalil's extended hand. Rachel shook hands with him without saying anything, just gazing. It took Jameela some time before she reversed course, and then she acted as if she'd known I had a Black cousin all along. She turned on her charm, saying that she'd always wanted to meet him.

I grabbed Jamal's arm and told Khalil that Jamal was my boyfriend. Khalil spoke to me in Arabic, letting me know that he thought Jamal was very handsome. I had to translate. Jameela then said to Khalil, "You don't need to shortchange yourself."

I managed to arrange the seating for our group with Jamal and Khalil in the center, Jameela next to Khalil, me next to Jamal, with Rachel next to me on the other side. I was counting on Jameela to continue finessing her interest in Khalil. It was Khalil who looked at Jameela and said, "I have to confess: My cousin managed to choose roommates as beautiful as she is." Jameela looked at him and said, "How kind of you. You're a true gentleman; do you take after your father or your mother?"

"I take after both, but mostly after my mother. She is half French."

Almost on cue, an attorney friend of Khalil's showed up. He greeted Khalil and started talking to him in French. I didn't want to show that I was watching Khalil and Jameela intently; I put my hand in Jamal's hand and rested my head on his shoulder, smiling with full satisfaction. Jamal pressed my hand and said, "You planned the whole thing. I think you're going to get him." When I asked who I would get, he said that he meant Moens. I smiled wider and gave Jamal a kiss on the cheek. He asked, "Did you also arrange for Khalil's friend to show up and for the two of them to start speaking flawless French?" I laughed and told Jamal that I wasn't a manipulator, and no one present was a robot. "No, but when you're challenged, you know how to play human chess," Jamal replied.

Reverend Pfeifer's speech at the church was enlightening, focusing on the efforts of the church to help the Black community in Boston. He said that he was particularly proud of his church involving itself in the struggle of other groups seeking equality.

That gave me an opening. I asked him how Black institutions in the United States, including churches, kept supporting the US government's actions overseas when they didn't trust the government's actions within the United States.

My question must have hit a nerve. He mostly rationalized Blacks' inaction by describing it as challenged and underfunded. My comeback to him was simple: "Statements of support don't cost any money." He smiled and agreed with me and praised my "intuitive" question.

At the end of the meeting, I approached Reverend Pfeifer and handed him my card. "Yara!" he said, looking at my name. "I like it." I said, "I hope to listen to you in the future."

"Does it mean anything?" he asked.

"Yes, it means baby butterfly in Arabic. I'm Palestinian, originally from Jerusalem." He then told me that he had been to the holy land and hoped to go back again. I told him that if he did to let me know, and I'd have my relatives show him around. I hoped that the exchange would initiate an opening for me to consult with him about the Moens dilemma. He shook my hand firmly as I left.

I was pleased to hear that he took note of my question and recognized my heritage, but I thought his comments were more polite than substantive. I said nothing about my exchange with Pfeifer to anyone after the speech. That evening we went out for dinner to an upscale restaurant. To everyone's surprise, Khalil insisted on paying for dinner. Jameela took note of that and expressed her gratitude.

Totally unexpectedly, Reverend Pfeifer called a few days later and asked if I could give a speech at the church. When I asked what he wanted me to talk about, he said, "You can talk about anything you like, as long as it pertains to human struggle. I presume you'll be talking about the Palestinian struggle?"

Out of nowhere, it seemed, I had found a potential new opening. I told the Reverend that his invitation couldn't have pleased me more. We agreed on a Thursday evening date four weeks later. It wasn't that I felt like a great speaker, although at Berea I had given a dozen speeches and presentations. I was thinking of two small challenges: what to say and who to invite, all for the purpose of enhancing my chances of cooperation with this Methodist church against Moens.

I decided to let everyone in my group know. Initially, I asked them to block the date and time, without telling them anything. All of a sudden, it dawned on me that my efforts might somehow conflict with Dr. Shahak's efforts, in case he was planning on contacting the NAACP again.

I asked Rachel if she could invite me to Pennsylvania to visit with her parents. She was more than happy to do so. She was eager to put me in a better mood. In Pennsylvania, I took the opportunity to speak with Dr. Shahak. "I'm giving a speech at a Black church in Boston," I told him. "Do you see any conflict with your efforts with the NAACP if I discuss the case about Moens?" He smiled at me and said, "My efforts fizzled, even when I gave them more details about the case. Unfortunately, they think we're trying to destroy the future of a young and bright Black man."

I had mixed feelings. On one hand, I was pleased that he didn't mind my discussing Moens's case in a public arena, yet his own efforts had led to nothing. He proceeded to ask me about my speech. I told him that I honestly hadn't decided. I was thinking of discussing the Palestinian calamity and relating it to Black struggle, but I was challenged as to how best to approach the subject. Dr. Shahak told me to let him know if I needed any help. I knew he was very liberal, yet it was a subject we had never discussed in detail. And it was an emotional subject.

For the following few days, and despite a most pleasant and relaxing visit with the Shahaks, I was nervous about how to approach my speech. Rachel offered her help, without knowing what it was about. Despite her open concern and willingness to help, I knew that I wanted to make my own choices. I just wanted to establish a direction, for nothing was firming up in my head. Rachel knew that whatever it was, it was of special importance to me, or I wouldn't have asked everyone to reserve the date. Dr. Shahak agreed with Rachel that the event was important to me, and that he knew what it was but couldn't tell.

As I was leaving, Dr. Shahak quietly said that he looked forward to listening to my speech, especially since we were both attempting to approach the same audience. His anticipated presence made it more challenging, because I needed to be more circumspect when discussing the Palestinian–Israeli problem. Other than Dr. Shahak, the others didn't have any idea of the exact venue, beyond the fact that it was taking place in Boston.

While in the past I'd declared defeat by attempting to withdraw from the battle, if worse came to worst, I was determined to go down fighting, a much more respectable posture. I decided to make a splash and attempt to define myself in more than one way. I wanted to keep it hidden from all, and I was thinking of a new initiative. For the past seven years, I'd consulted with the Allards, the Shahaks, or other friends—but this time I intended to do it alone.

Pfeifer had given me a wide latitude: anything that dealt with human suffering. I tried to put my thoughts on paper, and after several attempts I managed to come out with a complete outline relating the Palestinian struggle to the American Black struggle in many ways. I described the United States' support for Israel as a convenient way to cover up the West's, and especially America's, dereliction in helping the persecuted Jews of Europe during and after World War II. Similarly, I described how American society found it convenient to use Blacks as commodities to reap enormous economic advantages.

After some thought, I wasn't happy with my proposed presentation. I thought the link I was trying to establish belonged to another day and another venue. I was frustrated by my efforts. I thought my approach was too academic, and the theme too familiar.

I called Jamal. I shared with him that it was a speech that I was preparing—one that wasn't coming together. He suggested that I start with a famous saying or a poem and then try to format the speech in a way to either prove or negate such an introduction. While this idea would add another stylistic option, it didn't resolve the challenge of making the subject matter work.

I decided to take a shower. I took off my clothes and looked at my body as if I were trying to squeeze some thoughts out of it. Suddenly, a thought surfaced. I asked myself what I was doing, looking at myself in the mirror; I didn't recall observing my body like that before. Regardless of how I looked, above all, I was doing something new. I was revealing my own body to my own self. It was then that it came to me: Why not reveal my innermost thoughts to the audience, and then I could weave a narrative describing my thoughts about the Black struggle within the American context and independent of the Palestinian struggle?

I decided that it was a Black church with a Black audience in need of listening to my thoughts about *their* struggle, not about the Palestinian struggle. Maybe talking about the Palestinian struggle could come later. Then I revisited what Jamal had proposed, about starting with a saying or a poem. I first thought of a seventh-century saying by the fourth successor to Prophet Mohammad, Ali ibn Abi Talib:

> *If the righteous keep silent about injustice*
> *The unjust will delude themselves as being just.*

Why not attempt to unburden myself by revealing my thoughts to the audience openly and honestly, and let the chips fall where they may? I had nothing to be ashamed of. I wanted to be true to myself and be open with the audience. I wanted to find a process that covered exposing my thoughts, specifically about the struggle of Black Americans, which could also include a narrative about Moens.

I went back and forth about this idea. Then I thought, Why not use my own poem? I'd written six different Arabic poems that I'd shared with my father and Mira, and no one else. They were simple poems, because I couldn't reveal to my father my real feelings and thoughts about love and sex.

But I'd never written a single poem in English. I decided to write my poem in Arabic first and then translate it into English. For three nights, I confined myself to my room, eating sandwiches and drinking tea, to the extent that Rachel and Jameela were worried about me. When Rachel asked, I told her that I was writing an Arabic poem. She then asked if I could translate it for her and Jameela; I told her that I would, but not anytime soon.

I ended up with a poem that sounded acceptable to me. My worry was mainly my ability to translate it. I tried for a whole day, but the translation didn't flow smoothly. I was at an impasse. Then my father's words came back to me: that some poems could not be translated word by word; instead, only the essence and the main descriptions needed to be carried through.

I proceeded to memorize my new Arabic poem, and after I did that, I started writing a new poem in English. It contained all the meanings, most of the expressions, and the sentiments that my Arabic poem contained. To my own surprise, things started flowing. It only took me five hours, after which I read it over and over again. I was pleased: It even rivaled what I had written in Arabic.

Suddenly I felt a vacuum—a vacuum you feel after an accomplishment, with a sense of relief. I didn't know what to do. I smiled to myself and asked Jameela if I could borrow her tape recorder. I recorded my recitation of the poem three times. My recording sounded more impressive to me than listening to my own recitation. I wanted to bounce it off somebody but decided it was too risky and not in line with my desire to take completely independent steps. I decided that I should trust my own judgment.

It was only three days from the event. Whenever I could, I listened to the recording, and it kept sounding better. I hid the recorder in a locked suitcase, because I didn't want Jameela to find it and listen to the poem. I could see how both Rachel and Jameela were looking at me. They could tell there was a change in me. A huge burden had been lifted off my shoulders, and I was moving and acting in a nimbler way. I could tell that they wanted to ask about my change in attitude, but they held off doing so. For some reason, I wasn't concerned about my own performance.

The morning of the event, I told Jameela and Rachel that I was giving a speech at a Black Methodist church in Boston and asked them to ask no questions of me and to wait to listen to my speech. They said nothing and both nodded. Dr. Shahak and Jamal had arrived the night before. I told Rachel to share the address with her father and for Jameela to share it with Jamal. I didn't mention to anyone that Khalil was also going to attend. I told them both that I intended to go to the church by myself an hour early. I wanted to test the surroundings.

I could tell they were inquisitive; I could see it in their probing eyes. But I was intent on making my decisions totally independent of anyone's opinion, and I did. I didn't want anyone to give me any advice. I wasn't exactly sure what the reaction to my presentation would be, but I wanted it to be all my responsibility, all the way.

Chapter 17

I was met warmly by Reverend Pfeifer. To my surprise, there were around thirty people already waiting. I was loose and slightly animated. The speeches I gave when I was at Berea had prepared me reasonably well. I cased the hall and chose four points to set my sights on during my delivery. I liked the fact that the hall was twenty-two seats wide and thirty rows in length. It provided me with easier concentration spots. I took the initiative and approached the thirty or so audience members already present. I introduced myself and gave each of them my card, the same one I had given Reverend Pfeifer. None of them had any trouble pronouncing my name. They asked questions about my background, and I told them that I would be filling in some details, if need be, after the Reverend had introduced me.

Fifteen minutes before the start of the event, Dr. Shahak led the group into the church. To my utter surprise, he was accompanied by Annette. I ran toward her and hugged her warmly, shedding tears of joy. She hugged back and said in French, "Boston is an eye flutter away when it comes to my baby." We exchanged kisses and kept holding onto each other. I looked at Dr. Shahak. "Thank you for coming, and thanks for my mama," I said. For the first time, he said, "Don't I deserve a hug too?" I gave him a very warm hug.

The hall filled up with more than two hundred people. I recognized some faces from the faculty of Harvard. I suspected that there were possibly ten others from Harvard there as well. Despite this, I didn't feel nervous. Five minutes before the speech, Pfeifer told me to introduce myself.

"My name is Yara, and I want to thank Reverend Pfeifer for inviting me to address this fine crowd," I began. "But before I begin, I owe the Reverend a sincere apology. When we met at Harvard, I asked him a tricky question, specifically for the purpose of cornering him and for him to notice and remember me. I am afraid my devious method worked and here I am, having been invited to speak tonight. Again, I apologize, because I want to be honest and open through and through, for the subject I am about to discuss requires complete and unvarnished honesty and openness.

"My interest in Black affairs intensified after realizing my sensitivity about not having dated a Black person, while at the same time believing fully in the Black struggle for equality in the United States. I felt guilty. That was my feeling when I first arrived at Harvard, and as a result I sought to date a student I knew at Berea College; ironically one I didn't really like then. Unfortunately, I got more than I bargained for and in short order found out that he was Black in color only and completely lacking Blackness in essence. Not only that, but he has been successful through his career in achieving what he didn't deserve, and he is now about to take a very sensitive position with the NAACP, with an eye on the Supreme Court.

"This is actually why I went to listen to Reverend Pfeifer in the first place. I wanted to find an opening to connect with the Black community to stop this con man from executing his plan according to his most selfish interest, a dangerous plan, as he happens to be a self-hating man.

"You must have noticed that I didn't present my background to the degree I should have. This is because I want to reveal myself through presenting my thoughts and feelings about Black struggle. This is neither about me nor about the Palestinian struggle. I wrote a poem for this occasion to express my thoughts and views, all in English, for the first time.

"But before I start let me share with you a verse that belongs to my own religion. It says 'Do not begrudge what is beyond your control. It might prove beneficial.' Well, I have news for you. While I was surprised to have encountered and sought a sick man, I am pleased to say in public, and to share it with one special person and this fine audience for the first time, that as a result of one sad encounter, I have found love for a wholesome man. He is here in this hall, and for the first time I can say publicly, I love you, Jamal, with all my heart."

Jamal and every member of the group looked surprised. Jamal clearly didn't know what to say. His eyes were flooded with moisture as a broad smile filled his face. Jameela held onto Jamal's arm and rubbed it warmly and approvingly. Annette gave me an air kiss and one to Jamal. Dr. Shahak shook hands with Jamal. Rachel put her hands over her mouth and smiled silently.

A Harvard professor stood up and started clapping, followed by the whole audience. Jamal stood up and bowed toward the audience behind him. Annette continued to smile and gave me more air kisses. Within a couple of minutes, silence fell over the audience. I took a deep breath and sighed. I pivoted to look at the four spots I chose to alternate concentrating my sights on and started reading. Just about everyone in attendance had their eyes wide and ears perked up. Their faces transformed from expressions of joy to anticipation. I said, "Indulge me. I hope you don't mind; I am here lecturing myself and no one else. This is about my experience with race relations in America."

In my contemplation,
I felt the need for an explanation.
I am grateful and need not digress,
for America played large in my own progress.
Yes, sometimes I felt marginalized,
but where else an immigrant is not criticized.
My glass was more than half full
when I mixed and mingled and arrested all the bull.
I started slowly, occasionally accepting to be weak,
but soon I made them all feel
I am whom they needed to seek.
Within my comfort, I made choices
and moved from point to point,
to demonstrate my forces.
Alas, as this comfort gave me the time of day,
I possessed the luxury to voice my thoughts
and didn't care, come what may.
I nursed my neighbors and helped my friends,
and when rightly challenged I made amends.
With time I felt accomplished
and hoped my virtues to be replenished.

I felt that something was missing,

as my sight was near and many I was dismissing.

I labored to find my failing,

to finally locate the spot to which I was sailing.

I told myself I was too conventional

by looking at what was ethnic and traditional.

Who else, did I ask, deserved my sympathy,

and in no time, a revelation surfaced about my lack
   of empathy.

He is a man unlike me, neglected, trivialized,

and brutally locked up with an abandoned key.

Good god, I said, why I was blind for so long,

and why I didn't figure he was not able to belong!

I came from a far land,

and here I am aggressive in my demand.

Why does this man yearn to be equal,

and finds no resolution, with one after another failing
   sequel.

No said I, that can't be.

He created him as well as he created me.

God has always asked me to open my mind,

to appreciate that we are all of the same kind.

I am delinquent and need more than recognition;

I need a task with proper personal admonition.

I looked around and searched my soul,

to find out that I needed to make this challenge my call.

I sought to know where to start,

and the echo said that I needed the whole country
    to chart.

I looked at America to define its symbols,

and to avoid running into its chronic swindles.

Why not start with one that is recited without hesitation,

the national anthem, where I located my desired
    destination.

I started by attempting to discern its meaning over
    and again,

and once I finished, I ended with severe mental pain.

I tried to rewrite it from the beginning to the end

but failed to come up with a substitute to fend.

Just as an impasse converts into a resolution,

my creativity soon revealed a conclusion.

To change the anthem where it reflects conflicting
    applications,

through exposing the core and essence of my trepidations.

To express myself and shout out a distinct feeling,

to give the anthem, as if I were a Black American, its
    full meaning.

Whereby it leaves no distance between its words and
    its reality, to become a wordsmith's fulfillment of
    its actuality.

By stroke of a pen and a simple addition,

I altered it but kept the same rendition.

For the star-spangled to reveal its core,

I needed only to combine my thoughts

with my Black brothers' suppressed roar.
*O'er the land of the free, **but for me,***
*and the home of **no** brave without **recognizing***
my humanity.

I tipped my head down to confront the eyes of the audience, including those of my family and friends. The same professor who clapped when hearing my declaration of love for Jamal rose and clapped hard again. Despite his lead, the rest paused for a long ten seconds, and then one after the other joined him in a standing and robust ovation. Two other Harvard professors approached me and shook my hand firmly. Dr. Shahak gave me a cuddly hug. Almost half the audience shook my hand. Rachel, Jameela, and Annette all hugged me warmly. Annette kissed me on both cheeks and said, "I want a copy. I want to translate it into French. I have several professors at the Sorbonne who will do it for me."

At the very end, Jamal hugged me and wouldn't let go. He whispered in my ear, "I have to confess, I was concerned at first about you hesitating to ask me to accompany you; now, I understand. You wanted to surprise everyone."

For the first time, I talked to him in a new tone. I said, "No, my love. I didn't want anyone to take responsibility for my own thoughts and expressions. This is the way I feel, and this is the way I wanted to emphasize to everyone that this is how I feel. I hope I am more appreciated for my honesty about my own thoughts, whether or not they agree with me."

Jamal wrapped his arms around me and held me up and said, "You're not only my love; you are my star. You should have seen yourself reciting your poem. I would imagine this is the way the philosophers looked in the arenas of ancient Greece, defending their stands." As we were talking, Reverend Pfeifer approached me and said, "I thought I was taking a chance, but not at all, and I'm going to make sure you are heard in Black and white churches alike. You were magnificent and so courageous. Don't you think I want to say the same? I can't do it as openly and eloquently as you did. I would like to do it, but the system I belong to does not allow it. It almost didn't allow it for Martin Luther King."

I told him that my inspiration came from Martin Luther King and Fredrick Douglass, but that in this case it came more from Douglass than King. When Pfeifer asked why, I told him that I thought Douglass was crisper in his denunciation of the perpetrators than King was, and that I, too, had denounced the same perpetrators indirectly but possibly more saliently through my choice of the national anthem. "The same perpetrators want the instruments of their system to be sacrosanct but wouldn't allow people like us to analyze such instruments, and when you think about it, the national anthem, when applied to Blacks, is a sham," I added.

He then looked at Jamal and said, "This is the handsome man you were referring to! Well, he's going to have to work hard to keep up with you. You might be too feisty for just about anyone, including him. Listen, I'm willing anytime to meet and discuss the problem with the other guy." At that moment, I'd almost forgotten about why all of this was taking place. "Yes, yes, I am available anytime you are," I said. "And don't worry about Jamal; he is my compass." I gave Jamal a kiss on his cheek.

As usual, Dr. Shahak wanted to treat everyone to dinner. Annette said she couldn't conceive, under these glorious circumstances, of anybody paying for dinner but her. To my surprise, the ones who seemed to be most pleased with the event were Jameela and Khalil. I didn't know why, but I had my theory. I think Jameela thought I was a tease and that I'd drop Jamal and hurt his feelings. Now that she'd heard me in public, on a stage, expressing my love, she was pleasantly surprised and appreciative. On the other hand, Khalil strongly believed in kinship, and he was extra proud of me this evening.

Khalil really shone at dinner. He conversed with Annette in perfect French and told her that he had been married to a French woman but that she had died in a car accident. She had also graduated from the Sorbonne law school, and both went to Columbia to get their master's degrees. He had one son, living with his maternal grandparents in Paris, but he spent three months every summer with his father. It was his wife's wish that her son be raised as a Frenchman, and as such, Khalil was following her wishes.

Annette was translating her conversation with Khalil. As the translations took some time, Khalil took over and explained that he was still practicing criminal law, but to a limited degree. He was spending most of his time running his medical equipment business with Haiti. He told us that he got into it by accident. When he was an assistant district attorney, he prosecuted the company that was handling the medical equipment business with Haiti and managed to put the owners in jail. The federal government asked him to handle the business, since the United States government was paying for 25 percent of the cost of equipment.

Khalil talked to me alone and told me that after hearing about Moens, I shouldn't forget that he'd handled many cases similar to what Moens was doing and that I should lean on his criminal practice to help me out. I wanted to, but I was afraid that he might take a stance similar to that of Philip and insist on sticking to the most restrictive guidelines of the law. I kept his offer in mind, but I wanted to be freer to use even questionable methods, if necessary. Jameela's demeanor changed slightly when she heard that Khalil had been married and was raising a son. I could see a look on her face, a polite wait-and-see attitude.

All in all, after I finished my speech, I felt so unburdened by the load that was lifted off my shoulders, and also so pleased that my poem was so well received. I didn't feel like adding anything to what was expressed in the poem. I just wanted to relax by laying my head on Jamal's arm and saying nothing, but I didn't. Everyone noticed my cheerful attitude, and I noticed their congratulatory demeanor.

At the restaurant, I perked up when Annette ordered two bottles of the finest Gevrey-Chambertin. This time, Jameela was the one who volunteered to help. She obviously wanted to signal that the Moens problem was uppermost in her mind and that her interest in Khalil was much less. I told her that we weren't sure which direction we were heading in and that it would be clearer after Jamal and me visited with Reverend Pfeifer. She nodded in understanding.

The evening was enjoyable and so fulfilling that I couldn't recall another like it. Khalil was looking at me and smiling. He whispered in my ear that he wanted to talk to me after dinner, but I couldn't tell exactly what about. In the end, he was brief. "I want you to remember that I am your cousin," he said. "You can lean on me anytime you feel like it. I am here for you."

Chapter 18

Two weeks later, Jamal asked me to call Reverend Pfeifer. The Reverend asked us to visit with him. Jamal took the lead and explained everything that had transpired with Moens. Pfeifer expressed his offense at Moens's behavior, and, to our surprise, he said that he would try to help out if he could verify the story. We proceeded to show him the recording device Moens had installed in Rachel's car. We were willing to give him the phone numbers of everyone involved, but he said that a group meeting would take less time. We then arranged to have him talk to the group.

Reverend Pfeifer brought with him his junior pastor and his assistant. The assistant took detailed notes. By the time he finished with the group, he was totally convinced of our genuine concerns and sincerity. We told him that Moens had already started working for the NAACP and that the NAACP hadn't given Dr. Shahak a chance to present the case to them. Reverend Pfeifer said that he would contact the NAACP himself, through one of the board members. Jamal impressed upon the Reverend not to share with the NAACP any compromising details, such as our using Moens's own hearing device in an attempt to entrap him. He assured us that his first contact with the NAACP would be for the purpose of setting up another group meeting, whereby each one of us would try to corroborate the events we had shared with him.

Pfeifer managed to talk with the NAACP by contacting his friend on the board. The NAACP board members were very understanding; they decided to engage the services of an outside consulting attorney and have him fly to Boston to listen to us. They didn't want to use an in-house attorney, lest they be influenced by Moens.

The process went on for more than a month. As we were waiting to hear about the exact availability of the attorney, Reverend Pfeifer got a call from his friend on the board. He told him that Moens somehow heard about the Reverend's contact with the NAACP, prompting Moens to write a letter to the board claiming that Reverend Pfeifer and I had a casual romantic relationship. He also claimed that Pfeifer was a philanderer and while he couldn't present proof of our relationship, he could prove the existence of two extramarital relationships. He claimed that Pfeifer contacting the NAACP was no more and no less than him trying to accommodate me, Moens's spurned admirer.

We were confident that Moens's allegations were mere fabrications but wondered why he would offer to show proof of Reverend Pfeifer's extramarital relationships if they were false. What could he be up to?

Reverend Pfeifer was convinced that Moens was as evil as we had described him. He asked for some time to consider his options. Before Pfeifer had managed to come up with any new ideas, Moens contacted Amanda Pfeifer, the Reverend's wife, and told her that her husband had a relationship with me and with others, and he was about to present his proof to the board of the NAACP. He told her that Pfeifer had even invited me to make a presentation to the congregation. After she verified that my speech did take place, Amanda became convinced of her husband's guilt and confronted him in the church. He couldn't convince her otherwise, but she agreed to hear about the experiences of the members of our group.

Everyone was there, with the exception of Annette, who had gone back to Paris. Amanda looked at me with scorn when she first saw me. Although I was uncomfortable, I was intent on setting the record straight. I looked her in the eye and said, "I know that Moens Thomasson is very capable and intelligent but just as devious, and I don't blame you for having been impressed with his credentials and influenced by his story. But the fact is that I have had no other romantic relationship here in Boston than with Jamal Armstrong. Not your husband."

Dr. Shahak said, "Yara is like a daughter to me, and I assure you that what she says is the full truth. Nothing Moens told you is true." Rachel spoke next. "Yara is like a sister to me, and I can also assure you that her only relationship is with Jamal and nobody else." Jameela was the last to speak. She told Amanda that Jamal would have nothing to do with me if any of Moens's allegations were true, and that I was one of the most honest people she had ever met.

Amanda apologized and promised to confront Moens. I asked her not to do so and informed her that we wanted to use Moens's tricks against him, and that it would be better for him to be under the impression that Amanda was on his side. To our surprise, this request did not go over well. Apparently, Amanda thought that we didn't want her to confront Moens because he might present further proof of his allegations. She asked for further proof that what we told her was true, so we gave her the contact information for the

Berea graduates living in New York. She began to look somewhat convinced as we acted immediately by responding to her suspicions and giving her the New York contacts.

I took Dr. Shahak and Jamal to the side to suggest that we needed to guide Amanda somehow. They both agreed. Jamal asked Amanda if he, Dr. Shahak, and I could talk to her about how to approach Moens. She took offense at the suggestion. "I was working toward my doctorate when I married Don," she snapped. "I'm not a kid."

Within days, Amanda called to let me know that she had met with Moens. She described in detail what had happened. Moens was most cordial and deferential. He told her that under normal circumstances he wouldn't resort to such tactics, but under the current circumstances, he had to. He grabbed a folder and showed her pictures of two good-looking women in their early thirties. "I know that your husband had more than these two, but I am sure of these two—each had a year or more long relationship with him."

Amanda had also spoken with the three New Yorkers, and after her confrontation with Moens, she took it upon herself to visit me, Rachel, and Jameela. She was steaming and visibly agitated. She looked at me and said, "You're the snake in all this! Moens showed me pictures of two of Don's women; he has the goods on them, and he has the goods on you." I didn't know what to say. Jameela came to the rescue. "What kind of pictures did he show you?" she asked. "Did he show pictures of two women in the act with your husband? What exactly did you see?"

When Amanda hesitated, Jameela continued, "You come here on your high horse, doctorate or no doctorate, and accuse every one of us of being blatant liars. You should be ashamed of yourself. You owe Yara, above all, an apology. For the last time, I'm telling you that we and the students in New York are telling the truth. Do you have anyone else questioning our reputations other than Moens Thomasson? Why would you not believe ten different people against one?"

Amanda said nothing and turned around to hurry out of the house. But Jameela kept going. "Maybe *you've* had an affair and want to accuse the Reverend of a similar indiscretion. Tell me, am I on the right track?" Rachel and I were speechless. It was out of character for Jameela. Rachel pulled me toward Jameela and we all hugged each other. Then Jameela pulled loose and hurried out. Rachel and I thought she was going after Amanda, carried away by her anger.

Instead, Jameela headed to see Reverend Pfeifer. Two hours later, she came back smiling. "I might have gone overboard, but the Reverend confirmed that Amanda had a couple of extramarital affairs. He knew that she was trying to get even." Jameela continued, "Right now is the time to confront Amanda and settle the score in a polite way." When Rachel asked what she meant, she said that the Reverend had given her their home address.

When we got to the Pfeifer house, Amanda tried to shut the door in Jameela's face. Jameela stopped her and said, "We know everything. We're not interested in your affairs. We're not even interested in retaliating against Moens; we only want to stop him from using his position at the NAACP as a stepping stone to fight against a cause I cherish. And let me tell you something: Neither Yara nor Rachel are one iota less committed than me."

A moment of truth must have descended upon Amanda. She simmered down and acquiesced. She started speaking in a hushed voice and very polite manner. She asked us what we wanted. Jameela asked if we could sit down. In no time, Amanda agreed to be our agent against Moens and also agreed to take our opinions into consideration when she approached him again.

Moens was, again, one step ahead of us. He went to see Reverend Pfeifer. Initially, the Reverend refused to talk to him, but then he relented. Moens told the Reverend that he was willing to let bygones be bygones and that all what he wanted was to be left alone, and he'd promise to leave all of us alone. The two women whose pictures he had shown to Amanda accompanied Moens. They were introduced to Reverend Pfeifer as friends of Moens who were visiting him.

The following day, Reverend Pfeifer came over and relayed what Moens had told him. I told him to tell Moens that I was considering his offer. By the time the Reverend went back to the church, he'd found out that Moens had lodged a complaint with the Judicial Council of the Methodist church. His letter to the council included the names and pictures of the two women, each entering the church independently, as alleged proof that they were somehow involved with the Reverend. Moens had also sent a copy of his complaint to Amanda. At that point, Amanda had decided to extricate herself from any effort to help out. She wasn't confrontational, since we knew about her extramarital activities, yet she was adamant that she wanted nothing more to do with the situation.

I was totally at loss about what to do at that point. I had exhausted the help of my roommates, my boyfriend, Dr. Shahak, and Annette, and I had cost Dr. Shahak and Annette a considerable amount of money.

By then Jameela had simmered down about Khalil's prior marriage and the fact that he was a single father. She saw how disappointed I was at this latest development with Moens. She told me to cheer up. When I told her that I was worn out by the extent to which I had hurt other people who wanted badly to help but instead got let down and damaged, Jameela said that there was someone I was overlooking. "Who?" I asked.

"How about Khalil?" she asked. "If you're hesitant to call him, I will."

It was clear that Jameela wanted to contact Khalil for her own interest. When I told her that I needed completely imaginative and outside-the-box advice, not legalese dished out by attorneys and FBI agents, she said that I didn't know for sure that Khalil was not that kind of person. She was right; I didn't know that. I paused and told her that I would call Khalil and try to have him visit.

Jameela smiled; clearly, she had revived her interest in Khalil. I called him, and he was as gracious and warm as always, and promised to drive to Boston the following weekend.

Chapter 19

I arranged a four-person dinner, including Rachel. I didn't want to appear to be promoting a relationship between Jameela and Khalil, although I was. At dinner I shared most of what had happened with Khalil, giving Jameela a chance to participate in the conversation. To my surprise, Khalil was more animated and engaged with Jameela, in a casual and lighthearted way. Rachel said very little, by prior arrangement. Also by prior arrangement, Jameela summarized the whole situation and said, "Yara is hoping for someone who is creative and knows how to skirt the law without crossing it."

Khalil looked at me and said, "If this is what you want, why shouldn't you be the one to let me know?" It was obvious that Khalil was intending a double message: that he was willing to skirt the law, and that he was also aware of Jameela's interest. "If I come up with a scheme to meet your criteria, do I need to contact you or Jameela?" Jameela answered that he should contact either one of us, as we were both being challenged by Moens.

He looked at all three of us and said, "Nothing pleases me more than to be of help to my beautiful cousin or you, but if I become involved, you have to listen to me. I've prosecuted dozens of people with similar transgressions. If this is agreeable to all three of you, let me give it some serious thought, and I'll see if I can come up with something. And I mean all three of you, since I'll need your help."

Jameela jumped at this and said, "This is exactly what we've been doing! It's been a group effort all along, though Yara naturally has been taking the lead." Rachel tried to change the subject, lamenting the fact that Philip wasn't as much in the picture as she would have liked him to be. Khalil told her that he was still in touch with dozens of current and former FBI agents and not to worry since he could still count on their help. I felt good about the evening. Khalil took me to the side and said that he wanted me to come to New York the following month to meet his two brothers, Sammy and David, who lived in Florida and would be visiting him.

After dinner, we went back to the house, pleased with Khalil's response. As we stepped in, Jameela got a call from none other than Amanda, who told Jameela that the Methodist church Judicial Council had temporarily suspended Reverend Pfeifer, subject to a full hearing.

Jameela called Khalil at his hotel to let him know what had happened. Khalil told her not to worry and that he'd be back in touch in a few days to discuss his strategy. His words were too general to be soothing. Although he was our only hope, we couldn't tell what to expect. On the other hand, everything Khalil said exuded a clear air of confidence.

Three days later, Khalil was in touch again. We listened to him on a speaker phone. He said that the only effective way to deal with Moens would be to discredit him once and for all, and in a big way. He added that he hadn't come up with specific plans yet and that he needed more time.

Following our call, Jameela, Rachel, and I were anxious and tense, waiting to hear more details from Khalil. A week later, he called to see if he could come over the following weekend. When I told him that Rachel might not be there, as she planned to visit her parents in Pittsburgh, he asked whether Jameela would be home. I told him yes.

He came over while Rachel was gone. Again, he invited us for dinner, this time to a fancy restaurant. When Jameela said that he didn't need to go to such expense, he said that he didn't mind and actually was thinking of inviting us to New York, with a plan to go a super special restaurant. He said that he hoped Rachel could make it too, and that he also wanted us to meet Sammy and David. He added that he hoped Jamal as well as Philip could also be there.

Before the trip, we got word that the Methodist Judicial Council was conducting Reverend Pfeifer's hearing in a month. In New York, I met my other two cousins. They were as warm and sophisticated as Khalil. They looked more like me, with even lighter skin, as my half uncle, their father, was blondish, through his Turkish mother. Sammy in particular was interested in the case; he, too, was a criminal attorney, practicing in Florida, where he headed a firm of twelve attorneys and four legal assistants. He promised to help out as much as he could.

We wanted to attend the hearing but were told that we could not, as the hearing was confined to the accuser, the accused, and Amanda Pfeifer. We didn't know what to do. I suggested that maybe we could argue that since Moens was an attorney, Reverend Pfeifer deserved to have an attorney present too. We contacted the Reverend and presented the plan to him, which he welcomed. Khalil wrote the council a letter with compelling legal arguments. To our relief, the Judicial Council agreed to Khalil's participation.

Khalil said that he'd come up with a theory. He said that the gangsters he'd prosecuted tried to scandalize their enemies with the same illicit behavior they themselves used. He explained that he had a strong suspicion that Moens accusing me and Jameela of practicing prostitution on the side meant that he probably was using prostitutes for his own pleasure or possibly as a side business.

When I asked Khalil how this would change things, he said, "Just wait; before I join Reverend Pfeifer at the hearing, I plan to know every step taken by Moens and each person he is associated with." Khalil wouldn't share with us what he intended to do. This is when Sammy said, "I agree with you, and I'm willing to pay for one of the three private investigators you plan to hire." Khalil looked at him as if he was taking him to task for spilling the beans and asked, "How did you come up with this scenario?" Sammy just laughed. "You know I've always been able to read your mind, even when we were kids," he said. In the end, they agreed to split the cost of the investigators.

The three private investigators were on board the following day and started taking pictures of every person who came in contact with Moens, plus taking down their license plate numbers. Within two weeks, Khalil had thirty-one different names, with full contact information for all, including Rose, a very good-looking woman in her early twenties.

The thirty-one included the two women who claimed they'd had a relationship with the Reverend. This also included John and Stanley, two pimps who seemed to help Moens with his sexual pro-curements. Khalil thought that there were five prime suspects, with one surely assuming a double role. He suspected Rose, based on her looks and the fact that she wore very expensive couture clothes and drove a top-of-the-line Mercedes Benz. He suspected that she was sleeping with Moens and that Moens might even be acting as her pimp. Khalil hired a fourth private investigator to follow her in particular. In no time, the private investigator confirmed her illicit double role. He didn't share his methods with Khalil.

Khalil's next step was to prove that Moens was involved in pimping Rose. So far, what Khalil had was the fact that Moens was associating with call girls and, by inference, sleeping with them for his own pleasure—a crime, but not necessarily enough to discredit him. That wasn't damning enough, according to Khalil.

We were two weeks from the hearing. Khalil's dissatisfaction with the evidence collected thus far worried me. I was gradually getting more nervous. I consulted with both Rachel and Jameela. They didn't know what else to do. Dr. Shahak said that he didn't have any new ideas; neither did Jamal. Coincidentally, I happened to be reading the *New York Times* and saw a story about a man who had managed to record the conversations of his cheating wife and finally decided to kill her.

I didn't want to kill Moens, but the story reminded me of the fact that he had recorded us. I asked myself if we could possibly record Moens's conversations somehow. I contacted Khalil to ask him what the legal prerequisites were for this. He told me that I first had to secure court permission, which was rarely granted. I asked if he could try. He said he was sure it wouldn't be granted.

That night I kept thinking, trying to find a way to tape Moens. I thought about the husband who taped his wife's phone calls. At one-thirty in the morning, having tossed and turned since 10 p.m., I decided to call Annette. It was 6:30 a.m. Paris time. Annette was awake but was surprised at my very early call. I was straightforward with her. I updated her about the call girl activities of Moens and told her that I had already found a contractor who would tape Moens's calls for two weeks for the sum of three thousand dollars. His name had been mentioned inadvertently by Khalil. I told her that I only had one thousand and needed two more.

Annette promised to call me back within an hour. In less than fifteen minutes she called back and said that she didn't intend to give me any money and instead was going to engage the services of the contractor directly. She said if we were ever caught to say that I'd provided her with the name of the contractor thinking I was helping her spy on her cheating husband in France. When I asked why go to all this trouble, she said that taping others might be a serious crime in the United States, but it was not a high crime on the international scene; American authorities wouldn't waste their time trying to extradite her, and if they did, the French wouldn't respond. Even if the French did respond, she had enough pull to stop it.

I smiled to myself. I'd been afraid to ask Annette for help, and now I had her full and enthusiastic participation. In no time, I managed to connect the contractor to a Parisian private investigator made available by Annette. The Parisian private investigator fronted the whole scheme, thus putting another step between me and the commitment of an illegal taping. Daily tapes would ship to France and copies would be sent to me via Pan Am flights between Paris and New York.

After the taping had begun, we got our first opening with the fourth tape. A conversation between Rose and Moens was recorded that discussed Moens getting his cut. The client was a multimillionaire real estate tycoon in New York City.

At first, I couldn't understand what was going on. But after listening to the tape half a dozen times, I figured it out. The tycoon was eighty-four years old and partially invalid. Moens was the one making love to the young call girl while the tycoon watched and masturbated.

I called Khalil and told him what I'd found but refused to tell him how I'd found it. I only told him that my source didn't want to be exposed in any way and would deny any knowledge about the matter. Khalil said that he had to think about it. I also told him that the two women Moens was introducing as witnesses against the Reverend, Star and Sherri, serviced Moens's sexual desires while also being under his management.

Khalil called me back and said that he was going to try to corner one or both of them at the hearing. He wasn't going to introduce any witnesses other than the Reverend and his wife. "You and Jameela might be called, if absolutely needed," he said. Since the hearing had no legal standing, Khalil had to think of ways to escalate it to a higher level. He asked that the proceedings be recorded. After resisting, Moens and the two witnesses agreed, in writing, as a result of Khalil having convinced the Judicial Board members that recording the proceedings would allow the accuser and the accused to correct inadvertent mistakes afterward.

Later, Khalil told us everything that had happened at the hearing.

Khalil was after more than cornering Star and Sherri; he was trying to entrap them. He had sent the Reverend to a special cosmetics shop, where they added an artificial birthmark on his arm. The mole was clearly showing just below the short sleeve of Don's shirt. While waiting to enter the courtroom, Khalil made sure that the Reverend paraded himself in front of the two call girls so that they would notice the birthmark. Then Khalil had the Reverend change into a long-sleeve shirt and removed the artificial mole from his arm.

Moens started by presenting the pictures of the Reverend receiving each of the witnesses. He described the two pictures as depicting just one of the many visits each of the two call girls made to service the Reverend. Then Sherri and Star each took the stand and claimed that Pfeifer was an oversexed individual, who needed their services once or twice a week. They said that they enjoyed his company as he was not only a good sex partner but a refined and considerate gentleman.

When Khalil's turn came, he asked Moens and each of the witnesses if they would stick to their same testimony in a court of law. Moens and Sherri said they would. Star said she wasn't sure. When Khalil asked Star if she was lying while the other witness was telling the truth, she answered that she was telling the truth too.

"In this case, why would you not tell the truth to a court of law, if, hypothetically, it ever got to that?" Khalil asked. Star changed her stance and said yes. Khalil then asked all three if they didn't mind putting their promise in writing. Moens was concerned that his refusal to sign off would lose the hearing for him. He agreed to put his promise in writing, and so did Star and Sherri. Khalil had the relevant documents ready to be signed right there. He noticed a look of worry descending on Moens's face.

Star and Sherri testified that they'd slept with Reverend Pfeifer so many times they couldn't recall how many. They claimed it was all done at the Methodist church, in a special hidden bedroom. Khalil asked them if when they made love to Reverend Pfeifer they were naked. Star answered, "Sure, we were naked, and sometimes it took over an hour." Khalil asked Star if she had ever noticed any particular birthmarks, old wounds, or deformities on Pfeifer's body. "Not on his body, but the Reverend has a square-shaped birthmark on his right arm," she said. Sherri confirmed that she had noticed it too. Khalil looked at the Reverend and asked him to remove his long-sleeve shirt; there was no birthmark on his right arm. Star and Sherri looked at each other in utter surprise.

At that point, Khalil took a chance and addressed the members of the Judicial Board. "Under the circumstances, I would like to ask for your indulgence. Would you like to continue, or do you feel this is sufficient for you to reach a decision?" The board members asked for a recess.

When they returned, they asked Khalil if he intended to sue any of the witnesses in a court of law. Khalil confirmed that he was going to sue all the witnesses. They asked him when. "Within one week," he said. The board members said that, in that case, they would reinstate Reverend Pfeifer pending the verdict of the court. They declared the hearing adjourned until then. Khalil told the board members "You can have your own hearing afterward, and you would be allowed to use the evidence presented in court for your own conclusions." The board members looked at each other, and one of them said, "Yes, we will." Moens tried to object, but to no avail.

Jameela and I were waiting for Khalil outside the hearing room. After, he shook hands with Reverend Pfeifer and Amanda and assured them that the lawsuit would cost them nothing. He gave me the warmest hug imaginable, and I kissed him on both cheeks after he told us that the full hearing was postponed. Khalil also hugged Jameela, and she hugged him back.

Khalil intentionally didn't want to use the younger call girl Rose. He had her in mind to be drilled during the trial of the lawsuit. He had to collect evidence about her dual role. Khalil, Jameela, and I took a cab to the house, where we found Rachel. Only then did I realize that Khalil and I had been wrapped up in talking with each other, without sharing with anyone else. I apologized to Jameela for neglecting her and asked if she didn't think that Khalil's performance at the hearing was superb. When she said that it was more than superb, I said, smiling, "Why don't you give him a kiss of appreciation on his cheek?" She did, and Khalil responded with an approving smile.

The news was music to Rachel's ears. Rachel called her father and told him. He was also very pleased. I called Annette and spoke to her in French, telling her that our contractor did a great job and that the information benefited Khalil, who was able to then corner Moens and the two witnesses. Khalil overheard me. When I finished talking to Annette, Khalil looked at me and said teasingly, "My French isn't that good." I knew then that he was going to use all the information I provided him, without claiming that it ever existed or that he was ever aware of it.

To my surprise, Khalil was ready. The complaint documents of the lawsuit were all prepared, with the help of Sammy. There was still time in the day for Khalil to go to the courthouse and file the suit. Khalil didn't want Moens to file a lawsuit first and for us to counter. To be first was one of Moens's traits; he invariably took quick action in anticipation of the opposite party's actions. Khalil wanted to have the upper hand. The suit was extensive, accusing Moens of being a habitual violator, starting with his acceptance into Berea when he was too comfortable financially to be considered based on need. It then referred to Harvard, and how he wouldn't have gotten into Harvard if he hadn't graduated from Berea. The suit spelled out the transgressions he had committed against me, Jameela, and Reverend Pfeifer, highlighting the fact that he used his own managed call girls to level accusations against the Reverend to the Methodist Judicial Council. The lawsuit was intentionally expansive and most probably needed to be trifurcated. The purpose was to impress upon and threaten Moens with all his potential illegal activities, all at one time.

Chapter 20

It wasn't surprising that Moens initiated a countersuit within days. What wasn't expected was that Moens would sue Khalil personally. Moens claimed that Khalil had caused the death of his own wife by sabotaging her car. The suit was contrived, of course; the police had issued a citation against the other driver and laid the blame on him, all the way.

Two weeks later, Khalil made a visit to Boston. Jamal, Philip, and Reverend Pfeifer were there as well. Khalil explained that Moens knew that his lawsuit was frivolous and had almost zero chance of prevailing in court. But since he'd sent a copy of his complaint to the bar association, Khalil concluded that the purpose of the suit was to defame Khalil by inducing the bar association to investigate the accident, hoping to disbar or suspend Khalil. Moens also sent copies of the lawsuit and his complaint to the media.

In the three weeks since the lawsuit had been filed, neither the media nor the bar association had taken any action. I, on the other hand, received a letter from the Immigration and Naturalization Service (INS) asking me to go to their offices for an interview. Moens had sent a letter to them claiming that I was a part-time call girl. Once again, it was the nature of the claim much more than its potential harm that disturbed me.

Dr. Shahak came to the rescue. He consulted with his own attorney, and both believed that Moens's actions constituted blatant harassment. The first thing Dr. Shahak did was contact Pennsylvania Senator Scott to ask for his help. Senator Scott contacted the Immigration and Naturalization Department on my behalf. They hadn't looked into the complaint but advised Scott to have my attorney investigate the two pimps, and if either of them happened to have a criminal record, they would dismiss the case right away. It so happened that both pimps, John and Stanley, had multiple criminal indictments. The complaint was dismissed in short order.

Even after the complaint to the INS was dismissed, I was still upset. When Khalil heard about it, he thought that it could prove to be very beneficial. He looked at the record of the two pimps and found that Stanley had two ongoing serious indictments, one state and another federal, and was out on bail. He was about to have his day in state court. The first indictment accused him of human trafficking within New York State, and the second accused him of human trafficking across state lines. Stanley was exposed to potentially severe penalties and prison time in both New York and federal facilities. Khalil thought if we could get him a reduced sentence, he might share with us what Moens had put him up to. If proven as conspiracy between the two, Moens would surely be going to prison.

Khalil contacted his friends in the New York State Prosecutor's Office to see if something could be done. It wasn't easy, but when Khalil contacted the Federal Eastern District and connected with the right man, he was informed that Stanley was also about to be prosecuted in federal court. Khalil used this information to alert the New York State's Prosecutor's Office about Stanley's imminent federal prosecution and reminded them of the obvious: that the federal government had priority and was planning to start its case shortly. New York, as a result, accepted settling the case for a two-year prison sentence in exchange for Stanley's cooperation.

It was unusual for a civil case to be remotely considered in a plea deal like this, except that the arrangement wasn't official; it was carried out by the prosecutor who had recently been in the civil rights division of the justice department before accepting a promotion to move to the state of New York. As a federal prosecutor, he had been aware of Moens's lack of enthusiasm about a very recent specific civil rights case initiated by the NAACP. It was against a young man who looked clearly white, with a white mother and Black father. The young man was accused of refusing to serve several Black customers at an upscale restaurant.

The New York State prosecutors contacted Stanley and made their plea offer. To their surprise, and despite their best efforts, Stanley turned down the offer without even demanding a better deal and despite his attorney's recommendation to accept it. The prosecutors couldn't figure out why exactly he was so adamant to turn down the offer. When Khalil told us about what had taken place, Jameela, Rachel, and I told Khalil that Moens must have somehow conned Stanley into turning down any deal. Khalil agreed and wondered why it wasn't so obvious to the prosecutors. It turned out to be an oversight.

I thought that we had enough on Moens for a possible conviction. While I was still committed, I was getting worn out by the thought that I'd just about consumed everyone's patience, although no one wanted to show it. I gave our situation serious thought for a few days to see if I could come up with any solutions for entrapping Stanley.

I had no choice but to seek help from Annette. She was sure she was immune from any potential prosecution were she to be caught. Furthermore, she had clearly enjoyed participating in clandestine adventures already. I called her and explained what was going on. When I told her that we needed to use the contractor one more time—this time to tape Stanley—she enthusiastically decided that she would arrange everything. She never told me how much she paid the second round, and I didn't want to know. All I cared about was planning the whole affair with her in meticulous detail.

Within two weeks, the tapes were in my possession. While no names were mentioned, it was clearly Moens talking to Stanley. Within minutes, Stanley put Rose on a conference call to Moens. Dates were set and a venue was specified, at a reasonably upscale hotel. I knew well enough that we couldn't choose the non-approved tapes in a court of law, because they'd been illegally secured. I called Annette again and asked for another recording to take place, if and when the next opportunity presented itself, and for it to be delivered to me at an agreed-upon drop-off spot.

The reason behind this arrangement was to alert Khalil to have his photographer take pictures of Moens and his companion together. In a few days, I received another set of recordings. They were for three different dalliances between Moens and Rose, the third having just taken place.

In one of their conversations, Moens told Rose not to sleep with anyone else anymore and that from that point on she would be his girlfriend. My reaction was immediate: While we didn't know whether Moens had genuine feelings for Rose, we knew then that he valued their sexual relations. In other words, he cared for someone—a person who might prove to be his Achilles heel.

Per prior arrangement, my calls to Khalil were taking place within minutes of my having received and reviewed the tapes of Rose's meetings with Stanley and Moens. Two separate tapes delivered, one after the other, showed Rose meeting with Stanley and a latter tape showed Rose being warmly received by Moens. The first meeting was for the purpose of disengaging with Stanley and establishing that thereafter she would be Moens's girlfriend and for Stanley to cancel all other existing arrangements. The second meeting was to celebrate becoming Moens's girlfriend. On both occasions, Khalil had dispatched his photographer, who took pictures of Rose's departure.

Both Khalil and I felt that we had secured enough. Khalil decided to play it tough by shaking Stanley down to cooperate or threaten to hand him over to the State as a bail violator. Larry, a private investigator hired by Khalil, confronted Stanley. He told Stanley that he knew that Moens had advised him not to cooperate with anyone. He also showed Stanley both old and new pictures of Rose meeting with him, Moens, and other clients.

Larry reminded Stanley that he wouldn't be receiving any threats or help from Moens, since Moens was going to be booked soon. When Stanley resisted, he asked Stanley to accompany him to a phone booth with the plan for Larry to prove to Stanley that he could suspend his bail in no time by calling either the New York or federal prosecutors. Stanley tried to stall and asked for time. Larry refused and reminded Stanley that he had only two choices: cooperate or go back to prison. Stanley asked to be compensated for lost business. Larry answered with an emphatic no, reminding

Stanley that no one received compensation for lost illicit business. When Larry contacted Khalil, Khalil said that he could possibly secure Stanley a job counseling teenagers about the evils of prostitution and drug use. As it happened, Stanley was also a recovering drug addict.

The deal was struck, with the understanding that Moens needed to stay in the dark. When Larry asked Stanley if he was afraid of Moens causing him physical harm, Stanley said yes, and that he'd witnessed Moens beat a call girl so hard he broke her leg. When Khalil heard about this, he thought that it was another potentially incriminating case against Moens.

Chapter 21

Court for Moens's trial was set six months from filing. That gave us time to wind down and concentrate on our studies and finish our second year of law school in a peaceful fashion. Rachel, Jameela, and I decided to completely forget about Moens for at least one month. However, the circumstances of the feud with Moens were making it impossible for Jameela and Khalil to develop a relationship. Even my relations with Jamal had gotten somewhat distant, for all I could think about was the case against Moens, too.

I decided to reinvigorate my relations with Jamal and try and cement something between Khalil and Jameela. I invited myself to visit Khalil the following month. I didn't want to beat around the bush; I asked Khalil if he had feelings for Jameela. He said, "Now I do." When I asked him why now and not earlier, he said that he had finally managed to dismiss all of Moens's complaints and accusations against him in relation to his wife's death. While the press and media did nothing about it, the bar association had sent him a letter of apology for even filing the allegations.

I couldn't believe what I was hearing. Moens's case had engulfed my family's and friends' lives for so long. Khalil continued to say that, if agreeable to Jameela, he would like me to bring her along when I came to New York next time. I told Khalil that we could have dinner one evening but that I wouldn't see him the following two days, because I wanted to revive my relations with Jamal.

I saw Jamal the following day. He was gracious and most understanding. He told me that his feelings toward me hadn't diminished and that he wanted to give me space to fight my own fight and regain my self-esteem. I told him that I didn't want the ongoing turmoil to disrupt our relations, considering all the turmoil that was going on. But since the situation was dependent on the lawsuit, I could now relax and wait for the results. I was hopeful for a win but sanguine that I'd given it my best, should we happen to lose.

Jamal and I spent two wonderful days together. By the time I left to go back to Cambridge, I felt our relations were back on track. I realized that Jamal and I had planned to tackle things together, but working with Khalil had become so consuming that I'd neglected my relations with Jamal.

Both Rachel and Jameela could see how relaxed I was after the trip. I told Jameela how much I had missed Jamal and how wonderful it was to spend two days together. Again, I couldn't beat around the bush. I asked Jameela, "Do you have strong feelings for Khalil or not?"

Jameela looked at me and asked, "Is this a yes or no answer?" I nodded. "Yes, it is. Khalil has strong feelings for you. The ball is in your court, so what's your answer?"

"I want to make sure his feelings for me are as strong as mine before I say yes," she said.

I said, "Then we'll be going to New York together next month, with Rachel too, if she can make it. But I don't want to see either of you, since I will be spending all my time with Jamal." I smiled, knowing that they both understood what I meant.

The weekend in New York was as pleasant as possible for all three of us. On the way back, all eyes and ears were directed toward Jameela. She was coy and said that Khalil had taken her to the two best restaurants she'd ever been to.

In no time, the relationship between Khalil and Jameela developed. He took her to Paris to meet nine-year-old Tarek, his son. We established a pattern where every couple of months Jameela and Khalil, Philip and Rachel, and Jamal and I would get together in Cambridge and go out for dinner. Other than that, Khalil was methodically preparing for the anticipated lawsuit.

At that point, Moens was acting as his own attorney. Out of the blue, Khalil received a letter from Moens asking for a meeting. They got together in New York City. Moens proposed to Khalil that in return for dropping any opposition to me, we would dismiss our suit.

Khalil was suspicious as to why Moens hadn't proposed this over the phone. He told him, "Look, Mr. Thomasson, when you have a real proposal for a settlement give me a call, and when you do, bring two witnesses and I'll do the same." He paused and then continued, "My clients' lawsuit will not only cost you prestige and money, but it will also cost you your law license. So there will be no Supreme Court; there might be a supreme prison. This meeting is over. Good luck." Moens left, saying absolutely nothing.

Khalil came to Cambridge three weeks later to tell us what had happened. I said, "I ought to be happy at Moens's humiliation, but I'm not. He is a super vindictive man, and I'm concerned he'll attempt something else against you or one of us. He probably can't fathom the possibility of being disbarred and losing all hope of becoming a Supreme Court justice."

Khalil noted my concern but reassured me that he could easily stand up to any bully. Jameela said, "You have all the evidence against Moens now. Could you assign another attorney to handle the case going forward?" Khalil grabbed her by the waist and asked her not to worry. I knew then that his mind was set and unlikely to change course.

After we had dinner together, I lay in my bed thinking about what would happen if Moens tried anything else. A few nights later, it occurred to me that we could continue taping Moens's conversations. This time, the stakes were higher: If we were to be discovered, our lawsuit would surely fail.

Again, Annette was enthusiastic. She arranged things, but this time she chose to put an additional buffer between her and the contractor: This time she used two French private investigators. It was safer. We didn't need to present the questionable information in a court of law, and I thought we had some time before Moens would execute a new devious plan.

The first recording was significantly revealing. It was an attempt by Moens to hire an assassin, and the target was none other than me. I didn't know that until I received a call from Dr. Shahak, who asked me out for lunch the same day but requested that I tell nobody, including Rachel. As I got to the lobby, before entering the restaurant, there was Annette. She ran toward me and hugged me before I could say a word. She took a deep breath, sighed, and then started crying. I looked at her and said, "Anything happen to Antoine, to Jean Pierre?" She shook her head. "No. No, everything's fine. Let's go into the bathroom," she said.

In the bathroom, she told me about the tape and Moens's latest plan. I was speechless. Annette said that Dr. Shahak knew everything and that he was waiting for us in the restaurant.

In the restaurant, Dr. Shahak hugged me tightly. Annette suggested that I go to Paris with her. "What about my studies? I'm one month from completing my second year," I said. Annette looked at me and said, "What about your life, and what about mine? I don't think I can survive losing you. I'd blame myself forever if anything happened to you." In the end, we compromised. We agreed that Rachel, Jameela, and I would move to a hotel and not tell anyone. But what could we all do about classes? Jameela was graduating in a month. Dr. Shahak, again, came to the rescue. He contacted Harvard and advised them as to the potential danger we were facing. They promised to provide Rachel and me one security guard and Jameela another.

That evening, Annette, Dr. Shahak, and I arrived at the house unexpectedly. Rachel was completely surprised. Dr. Shahak explained the situation to Rachel and Jameela. They agreed to move into the designated hotel right away. Minutes before we left, Khalil called me and said that he had received a call from Moens asking to meet, but this time he wanted to meet with Khalil and me, ostensibly to apologize and to promise that he wouldn't seek becoming a US Supreme Court justice. Khalil said that it was a step in the right direction but still short of ceasing to practice law. I told Khalil that it was a step in the wrong direction and that he needed to get to Boston, to where we were staying, and spend the night at the same hotel. He was shocked when I told him why.

When he got to our hotel, he told me that he never thought that Moens would contemplate such a heinous act. He engaged the services of another private investigator, bringing the number to three. Jameela, Rachel, and I kept together except when going to class. We didn't want to split the two private investigators unless we had to.

In the morning, Khalil met with us, along with Annette and Dr. Shahak. The private investigators were nearby. Khalil said that we could use the tapes to alert the police, but we'd risk the consequence of violating the law, and we'd have to drop the case against Moens. He asked us to give him forty-eight hours; he had an idea and needed to test it first.

That evening he must have made thirty calls from the lobby of the hotel. He was speaking mostly in Creole. I could understand some words, as they were French. I could tell that he was asking people for help. Before we woke up the next morning, Khalil had summoned fourteen maternal cousins to New York. The private investigators told us about it later.

The following morning, at seven, the cousins headed to Moens's townhouse. When Khalil rang the bell and Moens opened the door, he could see all fourteen intimidating cousins in front of him. Khalil told him facetiously that he was leaving town and had decided to see him before he left. Moens figured that Khalil was there for another reason. After Khalil and Moens sat down and the other fourteen kept standing up, Khalil started his handheld recorder.

Moens was dumbfounded. He didn't say one word. Khalil told him that unless he followed his instructions, the tape would go to the police. He added that, in the meantime, there were six private investigators guarding us, doubling the number to discourage Moens from behaving irrationally. He relayed to Moens that his trigger man was cooperating with him.

He stressed that his conditions were clear: Moens had to resign from the NAACP, resign from the bar, and leave town and never come back. Khalil added, "I have here fourteen cousins and I have twenty-two more, and that's just on my mother's side; the others are all just as tall and just as big." Khalil then pulled out a *New York Post* clipping describing one of the fourteen cousins as having killed his girlfriend. Moens had no way of knowing that the cousin had been exonerated, since it turned out to be a false identity case, dismissed within three days upon catching the real culprit.

Khalil told Moens, "I expect you to call me when you resign from the NAACP, to call me again when you resign from the bar, and to call me when you leave town; and when you leave you need to provide me with a real address. By the way, Rose is staying behind; she is being booked on prostitution charges."

Moens looked at Khalil with a hollow look of a defeated man. When Khalil asked him if they were in full agreement, Moens said that he would abide by all the stated conditions. "Let me hear from you by 5 p.m. tomorrow then," Khalil said.

At 3 p.m. the following day, Khalil got his call. Right away, Khalil took a cab to the offices of the NAACP and asked for Moens. The receptionist told him that Moens had resigned and was no longer with them. Khalil pretended that he'd volunteered to help Moens on one of the civil rights cases. The receptionist introduced him to an attorney, who turned out to be the chief legal counsel. He confirmed to Khalil that Moens had resigned and gave Khalil a copy of the press release they had just written.

He made copies of the press release and proceeded to the hotel with all fourteen cousins. He phoned me and asked me and everyone else to meet him in a conference room of the hotel in Boston five hours later. When we all arrived, we were surprised to see Khalil's cousins. Khalil told us that he'd introduce them after his announcement. As everyone sat down around a huge conference table, Khalil passed out copies of the press release.

I couldn't help myself. I yelled in a very loud voice, "Is this really true?"

Khalil smiled. "Not only is it true, but tomorrow Moens is expected to resign his bar memberships and will cease to practice law anywhere," he said. Dr. Shahak had a dozen questions apparent on his face.

Khalil said, "Needless to say, I didn't convince Moens to resign; the tapes did, and all credit goes to the tape facilitator." Khalil told us we could all go back home and back to our normal lives but to keep the private investigators for another week, just to be safe. I said that I needed to go see my parents in Amman. "Being with them will be the closest thing to forgetting about everything here," I said.

Khalil said that he didn't mind accompanying me to see his uncle. Jameela said that she wanted to go too, and so did Rachel. So a few days after we finished our second year of law school and Jameela graduated, we flew to Amman. It was the three of us plus Khalil and Jamal. When Khalil first met my father, he bowed and kissed his hand. Most people in Jordan had abandoned this ritual. Khalil was following his late father's instructions and guidelines.

In Jordan, my friends witnessed a simple resignation to living in a refugee camp, challenged only by financial needs and the families' hope to one day to go back to Palestine. Jamal told me that he could sense the tranquility of my parents' home. The group stayed in downtown Amman, but they visited my parents every second day, after touring. Because I was their tour guide, after staying with my parents the first two nights, I moved into the hotel too.

By the third visit, my father was visibly relaxed, and I was at ease with my parents' simple dwelling. It looked the same as I'd described it to Rachel and Jameela. Unlike the first two visits, this time my father conversed in English. In his hesitant diction, he looked at me and asked, in Middle Eastern style, but openly, "When are you planning to marry?" The question took me by surprise, especially when asked in the presence of non–family members. Jamal was the only one who looked at me. The others, including Khalil, looked down. I didn't know what to say, not knowing what Jamal was thinking.

But Jamal was versed in religious and cultural affairs of the Middle East, and he wasn't surprised at my father's question. He looked at my father and, out of nowhere, said that he was planning to come back the following year and ask for my hand. Rachel and Jameela looked at Jamal and then looked at me. I just nodded my head. My father then looked at Khalil, who was at that point trying not to snicker, having figured out that Jamal's proposal was totally unexpected.

Khalil got up and spoke in Arabic, addressing my father. "Uncle Ayman, what Jamal meant is that he is interested in Yara, but he and Yara will think about it for a year to make sure they love each other." Khalil thought he was finessing a difficult situation. Instead, my father said, "When I married my wife, I had seen her only twice. What is this yearlong business? All Jamal needs to do is trust in God, and God will bless him and Yara."

I had to intervene, and said to my father, "Dad, you're embarrassing Jamal. He needs to make up his own mind and then I'll give him an answer. You can't force people to marry each other just because you want them to. They have to want to marry each other."

My father told me that I had become too demanding and to thank God that Jamal wanted to ask for my hand. I told him that I was always thankful and that I wanted to have children who came from a happy home. He said, "OK, when you become a lawyer, you'll work in Amman, and many male lawyers would die to ask for your hand."

Of course, I had no plans to go back and live in Amman. It had become too confining for my views and expressions. That evening, Jamal knocked on my door. "Listen," he said, "I know we've never discussed this, but if you're willing, I'm willing." I knew what he was talking about but pretended not to know. "Willing to do what? I told you that we can't be seen together alone in the same room."

"That's not what I am talking about, Yara. I'm talking about asking your father for your hand while we are here."

I looked at him and said, "Are you out of your mind? I don't want you to ask my father for anything. You need only to ask me."

"I know that," Jamal said. "But just to please your father."

I shook my head. "No, if we're to get engaged, it will be our decision, and my father will know about it over the phone or in a letter—end of story." Jamal looked at me and said, "Then will you marry me?" I told him that I earnestly hoped to, but there had to be an engagement first, during which we would talk about careers, children, and much more.

In the morning, I got Rachel, Jameela, and Khalil together and told them that Jamal and I had decided to get engaged for at least a year before getting married, but not in Jordan, only when we returned to the United States. Khalil looked at Jameela and said, "This is great! A year gives us time to decide whether we want to get married." Jameela looked at Khalil and said that he'd never even mentioned this possibility to her. He said, "I know; this is why we'll decide this coming year. Maybe we'll have a double wedding, or with Rachel and Philip, maybe a triple wedding." Visiting my parents—real people in a real, challenging setting—had helped loosen our emotions, it seemed.

We went back to the United States, where Sammy was following up with Moens. Moens had fulfilled the agreement to the last detail. He was no longer a practicing attorney. He opened a nondenominational Christian church in New Mexico, and from all indications he was doing extremely well. Within fourteen months, after Rachel and I graduated and passed the Massachusetts bar, all three couples got married in a single nonreligious ceremony—to the chagrin of my father and Rachel's mother. In time, both got over it, and my father was resigned to my living in the United States.

At the wedding I danced with everyone, but most of all with Jamal and Khalil. I gave Khalil a kiss and told him that he'd probably saved my life, and that otherwise I might have never gotten rid of Moens and married Jamal. Khalil looked at me and said, "No, I never saved your life or even got close to doing that."

I looked at him in confusion. "What do you mean?" I asked. Khalil explained that the supposed assassin, Jeffrey, had actually been working for him, initially to solicit the services of Rose in order to spy deeper on Moens. Rose apparently told Jeffrey that she was being harassed by one of her customers, and he was threatening to kill her. Jeffrey responded by claiming that he was a fixer, and that he could take care of things for her. She asked for Jeffrey's help and got it. Rose's customer was manhandled and forewarned. So when Rose shared her experience with Moens, he proceeded to engage Jeffrey's services as well.

When I looked at Khalil dumbfounded, he said, "I had the same plan you and Annette had. I would have recorded every statement and move Moens made if you two hadn't already done so. Your method was safer, having been channeled through France. By the way, the last person who paid a visit to Moens wasn't me: It was Jeffrey. He helped him pack."

My baffled look and reaction persisted. "I don't want you to share this with anyone," Khalil said. "My father told me before he died that since I was the oldest of my siblings, I had to make sure to take care of my family. He missed his Palestinian family so much. This was my contribution."

I went silent for a long time, and then said, "Not a word to any-one—not for a year. I can't keep it from Jamal much longer." Khalil nodded his head. I had mixed feelings. I told myself that now I had a third anchor, a family anchor to complement the anchors provided by the Allards and the Shahaks. Despite my travails with Moens, I felt so lucky, not to mention that I was marrying someone I so much respected and loved without reservation.

I looked at Khalil and said, "I think I want to dance with Jamal, and you need to dance with Jameela." He responded, "Yes, but don't forget that now you are also my sister-in-law. We need to see each other twice as often."

Jameela and Khalil decided to have no children and to have his son live with them after the age of twelve. Rachel and I opened a bio-patent legal office. It was called Shahak and Shaheen, as Rachel won the toss-up. Jamal and I decided not to start a family until I started earning at least $50,000. He was making $30,000 teaching at Amherst College. In the meantime, I started sending my parents $300 a month, with a plan of building them a new house.

We decided to call my first son Ayman, after my father, and our first daughter Annette. Rachel and Philip joined the Unitarian Church and decided to raise their children in the faith. Dr. Shahak gave her $200,000 as a wedding present. Both Dr. Shahak and Annette tried to give me and Jamal money as a wedding present, but we turned them down. Our excuse was that I wanted to have a chance to return some of their many favors and didn't want to accumulate more to have to pay back. Both Dr. Shahak and Annette relented but were chagrined about my rationalization.

In a year's time, we were all doting on Rachel's first son. She called him Joseph and decided not to give him a Jewish name. We initiated an annual gathering with Dr. Shahak and Sara, Rachel and Philip, Khalil and Jameela, Annette and Antoine, Jean Pierre and Josephine, and Jamal and me. The first gathering was in Paris, with all the pampering provided by the owners of exquisite boutique hotels. Many followed since and continue to follow to this day, mostly in the United States.

Acknowledgments

Coming from an upper-middle-class family, my gratitude goes to my parents, who had the foresight to have me intermittently live in a refugee camp in order to raise my sensitivity to a higher standard, by interacting and living with the poor and downtrodden.

About the Author

Wagih Abu-Rish is a Palestinian American author and activist. His novels are thematic, dealing with social and political issues pertaining to the Arab world. This novel deals with the challenges confronted by a female teenager brought up in a refugee camp trying to emancipate herself by reaching higher social, sexual, and racial standards.

He spent much of his career as a businessperson, specializing in acquisitions. During a long and varied professional career, he was a foreign journalist in Lebanon and an ad executive on Madison Avenue, in New York.

He has been active in promoting progressive causes, especially those dealing with the rights of women.

It is his hope that this book adds to his effort to highlight the themes he believes in. In it, he promotes the idea that most human beings tend to have a biased outlook on others, and only their education, upbringing, and intellectual exercise elevate them to an outlook of equality.

Mr. Abu-Rish earned his bachelor's and master's degrees in journalism from the University of Houston and University of Oregon, respectively. This is his fourth novel.

www.ingramcontent.com/pod-product-compliance
Lightning Source LLC
Chambersburg PA
CBHW050315110726
47899CB00007B/2252